THE VANISHING INDIAN

**Also by Zane Grey
and in Hodder Paperbacks:**

Wyoming
Sunset Pass
Twin Sombreros
Fighting Caravans
Wild Horse Mesa
Thunder Mountain
Forlorn River
Raiders of Spanish Peaks
Knights of the Range
The Lost Waggon Train

ZANE GREY

THE VANISHING INDIAN

HODDER PAPERBACKS

First published 1926
Eleventh Impression 1936
Hodder Paperback edition 1968

SBN 340 04371 7

Printed in Great Britain for
Hodder Paperbacks Ltd., St. Paul's House,
Warwick Lane, London, E.C.4
by Richard Clay (The Chaucer Press), Ltd.,
Bungay, Suffolk

CHAPTER 1

AT sunrise Nophaie drove his flock of sheep and goats out upon the sage slopes of the desert. The April air was cold and keen, fragrant with the dry tang of the uplands. Taddy and Tinny, his shepherd dogs, had wary eye and warning bark for the careless stragglers of the flock. Grey gaunt forms of wolf and tawny shape of wild cat moved like shadows through the sage.

Nophaie faced the east, where, over a great rugged wall of stone, the sky grew from rose to gold, and a splendour of light seemed about to break upon the world. Nophaie's instinct was to stand a moment, watching and waiting without thought. The door of each hogan of his people opened to the rising sun. They worshipped the sun, the elements, all in nature.

Motionless he stood, an Indian lad of seven years, slim and tall, with his dark face turned to the east, his dark eyes fixed solemnly upon that quarter whence the light and warmth always came. One thin brown hand held a blanket round his shoulders, and the other clasped his bow and arrows.

Nophaie's shepherding task was lonely and leisurely. He had but to drive the flock from grassy flat to sage slope, slowly on and on, and back again by sunset to the home corral, always alert for the prowling beasts of prey.

He was no different from other Indian lads, except that the dominant traits of his tribe and his race seemed to be intensified in him. His was the heritage of a chieftain. His mother had died at his birth, whispering strange and mystic prophecies. The old medicine men, the sages of the tribe, had gathered round him during the one illness of his infancy, and had spread their sand-paintings on a flat rock, and had marvelled at his quick recovery, predicting for him unknown and great feats. He was named Nophaie, the Warrior.

Nophaie wandered on with his sheep, over the sage and sand, under the silent lofty towers of rock. He had no cares, no needs, no selfishness. Only vaguely had he heard of the menace of the white race encroaching upon the lands of the Indian. Only a few white men had he ever seen.

Towards sunset Nophaie was far out on the open desert, with many of the monuments and mesas and masses of rimrock between him and the golden purple glory of the west. Homeward bound with his flock, Nophaie had intent eyes for the colourful panorama of sinking sun and transfigured clouds. The sun was going down behind broken masses of soft clouds, creamy and silver where the rays struck, golden in the centre of the west, and shading to purple where the thick, mushrooming, billowy rolls reached to the blue zenith.

A warning bark from one of the shepherd dogs drew Nophaie's attention from the sunset. A band of white men had ridden down upon him. Several of them galloped ahead and came round between the Indian lad and his home. The others rode up. They had extra horses, wild and dusty and caked with froth, and pack mules heavily loaded. Both men and beasts were jaded.

Nophaie had seen but few white men. None had ever tendered violence. But here he instinctively recognised danger.

'We gotta hev meat,' one dark-visaged man called out.

'Wal, we'd better find the squaw who owns this bunch an' buy our meat,' suggested another.

'Moze, you know it all,' growled another. 'Why squaw?'

'Because squaws always own the sheep,' replied the other.

'We hevn't time for thet,' spoke up the dark-faced one.

'Wal, we don't want Indians trailin' us. I say take time an' buy meat.'

'Aw, you'll say next let's eat hoss meat,' returned the man called Moze. 'Knock the kid on the head, grab some sheep, an' ride on. Thet's me!'

Moze's idea seemed to find favour with some of the band. The dominating spirit was to hurry on.

6

Nophaie could not understand their language, but he sensed peril to himself. Suddenly he darted out between the horses and, swift as a deer, flashed away through the sage.

'Ketch that kid, somebody,' called out the voice of authority.

One of the riders touched spurs to his horse and, running Nophaie down, reached a strong hand to haul him across in front of the saddle. Nophaie hung there limp.

'Bill,' called the leader, 'thar ain't no sense in hurtin' the kid. Now you-all wait.'

This man was tall, gaunt, grey-haired, and lean, with the eyes of a hawk. He scanned the sage flats to the pillars of stone. Neither Indian or hogan was in sight. Presently he spoke. 'Bill, hang on to the kid. An' some of you drive the sheep ahead of us. Thar's water over hyar somewheres. We'll find it an' make camp.'

'Nuh!' ejaculated the man Bill, in disgust. 'Talkin' about sense, what's the idee, cap, packin' this heavy kid along?'

'Wal, it ain't decent to kill him, jest fer nothin', an' it is sense to keep him from gettin' back home to-night.'

'All right, you're the boss. But I'll eat sage if them Indians don't track us, jest the same.'

'Bill, you're a bright fellar,' retorted the other. 'Mebbe this kid's family will find our tracks by to-morrow, but I'm gamblin' they won't.'

Nophaie hung limp over that horse for several miles before he was tumbled off like an empty sack. The band had come to a halt for the night. Nophaie's hands and feet were bound with a lasso. He heard the bleating of the sheep, and then the trampling low roar of their hoofs as they were driven off into the desert. One of the men gave him food and drink; another covered him with a blanket. Nophaie's fear eased, but there was birth of a dark heritage of hate in his heart. He did not sleep.

At daylight the band was off, riding hard to the southward, and Nophaie had no choice but to go with them. Towards nightfall of that long day the spirits of the men appeared to rise. They ceased to look back over the rolling ridges of purple sage, or down the leagues of cedar aisles. They avoided the Indian hogans and sheered off well-trodden trails. Next day some of the band were in favour of letting Nophaie go free. But again the leader ruled against them.

'Reckon it's tolerable lonely along hyar. We don't want the kid to be lost an' starve.'

About noon-time one day later they let Nophaie go free, and pointed down a road towards an Indian encampment. Then in a cloud of dust they trotted on. Rough but kind they had used him, unconscious of their hand in his destiny. But Nophaie never reached the Indian hogans. Another party of white people, of different look and voice, happened upon him. They were travellers of leisure, seeing the West, riding across the reservation. They had wagons and saddle horses, and Western men to care for them. Again Nophaie ran, only to be caught by one of the riders and hauled before the women of the party.

'What a handsome Indian lad!' exclaimed one.

'Let us take him along,' said another.

An older woman of the group, with something more than curiosity in her face, studied Nophaie for a moment. She, too, was kind. She imagined she was about to do a noble thing.

'Indian boy, I will take you and put you in a school.'

They took Nophaie with them by force. They took him out of the desert and far to the east.

And Nophaie lived and studied in the white man's school and college for eighteen years.

CHAPTER 2

As the train neared the Western town which was her destination, Marian Warner realised that this ride was not a dream, but the first act of the freedom she had yearned for, the first step in her one great adventure. All the excitement and audacity and emotion that had been her undoing now seemed to swell into a thrilling panic.

Long days of travel had passed since she had boarded the train at Philadelphia. The faces of friends, of her aunt – the few who loved her – had grown dim, as if every revolution of the wheels had deadened memory as well as lengthened miles. Little had she guessed how she had cut herself adrift. But to the last she had kept her secret.

Then, as many times during this long ride, she had recourse to the letter that had influenced her to come West.

> OLJATA (Moonlight on the Water),
> Feb. 10, 1916.

'DEAR MARIAN,

'Your letters and gifts were welcome as May flowers. I did not get them at Christmas time because I did not ride into Kaidab. The weather then was cold and I had my only living relative to look after. He was ill. He is better now.

'I rode the ninety-odd miles to the post between sunrise and sunset, over a trail known only to Indians. And all the way I thought of you, of the love for you that only strengthens with distance and time. Remembering your fondness for horses and how you used to long for wild and lonely places, I wanted you to be with me.

'But in spite of the joy that came with your remembrances, my ride back from the post was full of bitterness. I was again brought into contact with the growing troubles of my tribe, and with the world of white men which I have given up.

'Marian, my people now are very prosperous. The war has brought false values. Wool is fifty cents a pound. Horses and sheep bring higher prices than any Indians ever dreamed of. They think this will last always. They will not save. They live from day to day, and spend their money foolishly. And when the reaction comes they will be suddenly poor, with the trader's prices for food and clothing higher than ever.

'I have been here nearly a year now, and have yet to find one single Indian who is really a Christian. I have gone all over this part of the reservation. The Indians tell me there have been many good missionaries among those sent out here. White men who were kind, who studied the Indians' need, who helped them with their hands, who might in time have won their confidence. But for some reason or other they never remained long enough.

'And we greatly need help. Come out to the reservation and work for a year or two among my people. It could not hurt you. And you might do much for them. You could be a teacher at Mesa or one of the other schools. None would ever know that you came for my sake.

'Your letters heaped upon me terms of reproach. Marian, I have not forgotten one moment of our summer at Cape May. I live over every meeting with you. I love you more than I did then. It seems I am old now. Wisdom came to me here in my desert home, under the shadow of old Nothsis Ahn. I was born under this great mountain. When a boy I was stolen from my home under its red walls. And after eighteen years I have come back. I burned my white man's clothes and books – even the records of my football games – all except your picture. I put on buckskin and corduroy and silver. I seldom speak English and I am again an Indian. No more Lo Blandy, but Nophaie!

'I was young and full of fire that summer at Cape May. I drank the white man's liquor, Marian. I was praised, feted, sought because I had become a famous athlete – the football

10

and baseball player, winner of so many points against the great colleges. I danced and played the same as white college men.

'Then I met you, Marian. You were different from most of the white girls. I loved you at sight and respected you when I knew you. I stopped drinking for you. And for an Indian to give up whisky, once he knows its taste, is no small thing. I loved a white girl. I called you *Benow di cleash*, the white girl with blue eyes. And I'm sure your influence kept me from the fate of more than one famous Indian athlete – Sockalexis, for instance, who ruined career and health in one short year.

'But when I returned to my people the great change came. Not in my love for you, but in my youth. I am a man now, old as these sage hills, and I've learned from them. It was selfish and wrong for me to run after you, to love you, to take your kisses – wrong though it was, the best influence of my life. I am an Indian.

'Then, once here, whatever wild dreams I may have had were forgotten. I see the life of my tribe as a tragedy. The injustice to them is the blackest of white men's baseness. The compulsory school system for the Indian boys and girls has many bad points. The bad missionary is the apostle of hate and corruption. His ways are not the ways of the good missionary. I am an educated Indian – a chief in my tribe. I see their misery. I see them vanishing. I cannot marry an Indian girl, because I love you. I cannot have a child, because I love you. I cannot know any woman because I love you. When an Indian loves he loves for ever. It is infinitely easier for an Indian to love a white woman than for her to love him. I don't know why.

'So, Marian, I am here, no longer Lo Blandy, but Nophaie. My name means Warrior. The red sand I tread is part of the bones and flesh of my ancestors. I will live my life here and mingle my bones with theirs. I will do all I can for them. But alas! the eighteen years' education forced upon me by the whites enables me only to see the pitiful state and the doom of the Indians.

11

'Come, Marian, to Oljato – come to help me awhile or just to see the wildness and beauty of my home, so that always afterwards your memory will be full of the colour and music and grandeur and fragrance of the Indian land.

NOPHAIE.'

Marian put the letter away, conscious only at that moment of her emotions. Every perusal of it seemed to glean new sensations of pain, regret, sweetness and love, and awe.

'Nophaie, the Warrior,' she soliloquised dreamily. 'Somehow it suits him.'

She recalled the first time she had ever seen him. It was at Cape May, where a group of college men maintained baseball games with visiting teams, professional and otherwise. Her aunt, with whom she lived, and most of her Philadelphia friends, always spent some weeks at the seashore. And Marian enjoyed games and bathing and dancing as well as anyone. One summer afternoon a friend took her to the athletic field and pointed out the famous Indian star. How curious she had felt! There was a strange pain in the recall of that first sensation. Her eyes fell upon a tall bareheaded athlete, slenderly yet powerfully built, his supple form broadening wide at the shoulders. His face was dark, his hair black as coal. Striking and handsome as he was, it was not his appearance alone that thrilled her so. She was a thoroughly modern young woman and had seen her share of college games. In action the Indian was simply beautiful. He had earned his great fame as a football star, and had been picked by experts for the All American team three successive years. But he did not need to be so great a baseball player to be good to look at. He played an outfield position, and the chances of the game fell so that he had little to do except run. And his running grew more and more thrilling to Marian. How easily he moved – what a stride he had! Marian found she was not alone in her admiration. This Indian athlete did not need her applause. Towards the end of the game, at a critical time for the home team, he hit a ball far beyond the reach of the opposing fielders. The crowd roared its delight. The Indian dashed down towards first base, and, turning, appeared to gather speed as he ran. Marian felt the pound of her heart, the sudden shock of delight and pride in the Indian's sheer physical prowess. He ran as the Greek runners must have run, garlanded for their victories. How fleet! How incredibly faster and faster! Then he was making the turn for home base, and the crowd was yelling wildly. He seemed to be facing Marian as he sped on, magnificent in his action. He beat the throw and scored his home run, a feat the audience applauded with prodigious abandon. Marian then became aware that she, too, had been rather undignified.

That night at a dance one of Marian's friends had asked her:
'Have you met Lo?'
'Lo! and who's he or she?' queried Marian.
'He's the Indian crack. You saw him play to-day. Lo Blandy.'

And so it came about presently that Marian found herself facing the Indian athlete she had admired. Not just then had she realised it, but the truth was she had fallen in love with him at first sight. Something in her nature, never dreamed of before, went out to the Indian. He had a fine face, dark and strong, with eyes of piercing blackness. There was something noble in his stature, or the poise of his head, or the eagle look of him.

'Will you dance with me?' he had asked, and appeared as much at his ease as any of the college men.

Marian found herself dancing with an Indian – a very strange and momentous circumstance, it seemed. Evidently he had not made dancing one of his college courses, as most young men made. But he was light and strong; he carried her on without the bold contact so prevalent among most dancing men; and so Marian enjoyed that dance.

They met again by accident on the beach, and because no one else came and they were interesting to each other, they talked for long. After that day Marian went to all the baseball

13

games. And Lo Blandy became one of her numerous admirers, to the amusement of her aunt and friends.

But these meetings had been deadly earnest for Marian. She loved the Indian. She fought against herself – then surrendered and fought no more. He had more principle and better habits than any white boy she knew. So that summer, in the cool amber-lighted mornings by the seashore and on the moonlit nights when dance and music held their sway, Marian quaffed the spiced magic draught of love.

She wondered if she had as true and steadfast a nature as the Indian? Would she love once and once only? Vain queries. She loved now and that was all of pain.

Marian gazed out of the train window at the scenery. The farther she travelled the more untrue her situation seemed. Yet she was glad. A deep feeling within her stirred to strange promptings. She strove to justify her action in her own eyes. Surely one flight of freedom need not be denied her. The laxity of Marian's social set in no wise gave her excuse for wildness and daring. She hated the drinking and smoking of women, the unrestrained dances, the lack of courtesy, the undeniable let-down of morals. She had welcomed an opportunity to escape from that atmosphere. Outside of love for Lo Blandy or an earnest desire to help his people there had been a trenchant call to some subtle innate wildness in her. The prairie, the mountain, the sea, the desert all called to her with imperious voice. Some day she would surely have listened.

'I have no close family ties,' she said to herself, in sincere defence. 'I am twenty-three. I am my own master. I've always dreamed of love with honour – of marriage with children. Perhaps in vain! My aunt, my friends, would call me mad. They do not understand me. I am not throwing my life away. I can do good out here. I can help *him*. . . . Nophaie – what a strange, beautiful name! . . . I am not rich. But I have some money, and that I will gladly use now. Let the future take care of itself.'

So she settled the matter of perplexity and of conscience,

and gave up to the singular appeal of the prospect before her. Always Marian had yearned to do something different, unusual, big. She had travelled a little, taught school, tried journalistic work, and had one short weakness for dramatics. And she knew she had accomplished nothing. Here indeed was the bright face of adventure, mysterious and alluring, coupled with a work she might make uplifting and all-satisfying.

Flagerstown, the first Western town Marian had ever been in, was not at all like what she had imagined it would be. Her impressions of the West had come from books and motion pictures, which mediums, she was to learn, did not always ring true to life.

It was a thriving little city, bustling with motor-cars and active over its lumber, railroad, and cattle interests. It bore no signs of the typical frontier town. What surprised Marian a little was the fact that neither hotel proprietor nor banker, post-office official nor clerk in the store, nor a cattleman she chanced to address showed any curiosity concerning her. When she made inquiry about the Indian reservation she simply stated that she was interested in Indians and might do some journalistic work out there. Marian was compelled to confess that these Western men did not seem to be impressed with her. They were courteous and kindly, yet somehow aloof. It was a novelty to her. In the East she had endlessly been confronted with the fact of her femininity and youth and attractiveness. Here she seemed to catch a breath of life not thick and heavy with the atmosphere of sex. The West was young, virile, open. Already she began to feel free of fetters that had weighed upon her.

She ascertained that a mail-carrier left Flagerstown twice a week for the places on the reservation – Mesa, Red Sandy, and Kaidab. And the post-office man was kind enough to engage passage for her. Next morning the hotel porter called to take her baggage. Marian saw the most dilapidated Ford car that had ever come before her vision. What there was of it appeared to be wired and roped together. And it was loaded heavily with mail-bags, boxes, and sacks. There was a coop containing some chickens going by parcel post. Next to the driver's seat had been left a small space, evidently for Marian.

'Goodness!' ejaculated Marian, as she surveyed this doubtful contraption. 'Will it hold together? Is it safe to ride in?'

'Why, miss, sho thet Injun will get you thar,' replied the porter.

'Indian! Is the driver an – Indian?'

'Yes-sum. An' sho blowin' snow er sand makes no difference to him.'

Marian could have laughed, in spite of her uneasiness. But all she could do was to gaze helplessly at that machine. Then appeared a young man in ragged dark suit. His small feet were encased in brown buckskin moccasins with silver buttons. His dark face appeared to be half hidden by a black sombrero. She could see that he was young. She noted his hands as they slipped over the wheel – dark, thin, nervous, sinewy hands, well formed and mobile. Then he got into the driver's seat and looked up at her. He was only a youth. His face was keen, smooth as silk, without a line, dark as bronze. He had a level brow and eyes black as night. Suddenly they gleamed with intelligence and humour. This Indian sensed her consternation.

'You ready go?' he queried, in intelligible English. The tone of it gave Marian a little shock. Something about it, the low pitch or timbre, recalled the voice of Lo Blandy.

'Y-yes, I guess so,' faltered Marian. Dare she trust this frightful junk heap of a car and its Indian driver on a long desert journey? Marian's Eastern compunctions did not die easily.

'You go Kaidab?' asked the driver.

'Yes,' replied Marian.

'I get you there – five o'clock,' he returned, with a smile. It seemed a flash of understanding. He read her mind, and wished to reassure her. Marian's new spirit revived with a rush. She

16

had burned her bridges behind her.

'Will it be cold?' she asked, as she was about to climb into the car.

'You need blanket for while,' he said.

Marian had no blanket, but she had brought a heavy coat which would serve as well. This she put on. Then she squeezed into the small space beside the driver. The grinning porter called, 'Good night!' which dubious farewell in no wise diminished Marian's concern.

The Indian driver moved something that made the rickety car crack like a pistol and lurch forward. Marian could not stifle a gasp. The square-fronted buildings with their queer high board signs began to speed back out of her sight. Ahead the white asphalt road merged into one of dark earth, and there appeared a long slope of pine trees. Cold, keen, biting wind fanned Marian's cheeks. It nipped with its frosty breath. And it brought a strange dry fragrance. The car passed the line of buildings, and to the left loomed a mighty green-and-white mountain mass that hid its summit in gloomy rolling clouds.

'Storm,' said the Indian. 'We hurry so get 'way from snow.'

If anything more were needed to complete Marian's demoralisation, she had it in the gathering speed of that car. It belied its appearance.

'Oh! if they could see me now!' she murmured, as she snuggled down into the warm coat and peeped out at the wonderful green slope of forest. She thought of those at home who would have looked aghast at her boldness. Perhaps this was the moment of severance. Whatever it was, above all Marian's misgivings and defiance there pealed a subtle voice of joy.

CHAPTER 3

THE road upon which the Indian was driving led out into a pine forest, between the stately trees of which she caught glimpses of cloud-enshrouded mountains.

The cold, the raw wind, the increasing gloominess of the day, with its ominous threat of storm, in no wise checked Marian's momentary enthusiasm and awakening joy for the open country. She must see all, feel all, experience all with every sense acute. For as long as she could remember she had been cooped up in a town. And in her heart love of nature had been stultified. At last! She breathed deeply of the keen air. And the strong pitchy smell of pine began to stimulate her.

'What mountains?' she asked.

'Spanish Peaks,' replied the driver.

She asked him other questions, to which he gave brief and unsatisfactory reply. Perhaps it took all his attention to keep the car in the road. Besides, it made such a rattle and clank that conversation was really not easy. Marian ceased asking questions.

The road led through a forest of pines such as Marian had never seen, wonderfully fragrant and exhilarating after the cities and railroads. The grass was dead, bleached white, but the green of the pines gave relief to her eyes. Ten miles of forest the car traversed, then an open valley, fine ranch country Marian judged, from which view of the mountain range was magnificent, and then it entered forest again, with the difference that the ground appeared to be all cinders. The car chugged uphill, losing much of its velocity.

From a ridge top Marian's eyes were greeted by a strange and desolate spectacle – a wide black valley, a slope of black cinders, and a stream of red lava crusted and jagged, and beyond these foothills of black cinders smooth and steep, all waved and ridged like sand dunes carved by wind. A line of pines crested the first hill, and under this green stretch was a long bank of snow, its pure white contrasting markedly with the ebony cinders. A range of these foothills rose off towards the south, growing higher and smoother, weird and sinister monuments to the havoc of volcanic action in the ages past. Beyond and above this range towered a mountain of cinders, strangely barren, marvellously coloured in purple, black, and red.

Marian saw so much in this scored and devastated region that she regretted passing on so rapidly. Soon her Indian guide reached a down grade in the forest, ran out of the cinder zone upon hard road again, and here Marian feared every flying mile would be her last.

By and by the pines began to decrease in size and grow farther apart, so that glimpses of open country came to Marian. Then from round a rocky ridge quite abruptly the car sped out into thin forest from which stretched a vast waste of grey. The desert! Marian did not try to repress an exclamation of delight and awe.

She feasted her eyes, trying to grasp what it was that she saw. Moments and miles passed, and suddenly a grey squall of rain and snow swooped down from behind, enveloping the car. It brought a piercing cold. What rain there was soon changed to sleet. It pelted Marian, many hailstones bouncing off the glass wind-shield to sting her face. Gloves and pockets appeared little protection against such cold. Marian suffered. Her cheeks, her nose, her ears seemed to congeal to ice. The world around that car was white, swept by a blizzard, with snow fleeting across the ground. The sky was obscured. When Marian opened her eyes, at intervals, she could not see far in front of the car. This obscurity did not deter the Indian from driving fast. So that between her pangs and fears Marian had to make heroic enjoyment out of this hour.

At length the grey cloud lightened, the snow thinned out,

and the blue of sky shone through a thin haze of white. That, too, faded or melted away, and then the storm veered, leaving clear a great open space above. Marian grew aware that she was now far down in the desert, with open bare ridges all around her and the distant prospects out of view. The snow failed. The earth changed its white-and-black hue to a dull red. Once again the car sped out upon a height from which Marian had a second look at the leagues of desert. Here the immense reach and slope struck her more forcibly, and especially the great volume of light.

Once the Indian stopped the car, to examine some of its mechanism. Thus Marian was enabled to get out, to stretch her cramped, cold limbs. After that, when the journey had been resumed, she soon grew comfortable under a warming sun, and at length forgot both pangs and fears in absorption of this desert land. Her driver travelled downhill for no less than three hours. This brought them to what seemed an incongruity – an iron bridge spanning a rock-walled gorge, through which ran a muddy stream. Here in this valley the sun was hot. Marian had to remove the heavy coat.

Beyond the river stretched a gravelly plain, hard packed by wind, and its slow ascent at last gained another height, from which Marian confirmed her wondering expectations. Three level benches of coloured desert, as high as mountains, lifted their wondrous reds and purples and greys and golds towards the blue sky.

The ensuing hour, during which the Indian driver crossed the bare plains of sand and gravel and climbed the successive steps of coloured rock, passed by all too quickly for Marian. The sun beat down hot. To the north, in the direction the car was heading, more storm clouds were gathering. Above the last desert step the earth appeared a place of ruin and decay, a zone of sinister red and strange drab, where rocks and clay had been weathered into fantastic shapes. Marian likened the region to an inferno. Soon it lay behind, and she found herself confronted with a wide valley between glaring walls of rock. Dark rich green fields of alfalfa formed the floor of this valley, making the hot walls of stone naked and stark by contrast. Marian saw clusters of trees beginning to show green, and the roofs of two flat houses.

'What's this place?' she inquired.

'Copenwashie,' replied the Indian.

'Are those green fields Indian farms?'

'Some are. White people got most land now.'

'But isn't this a reservation for the use of Indians?' went on Marian curiously.

All the reply she received was a grunt of disgust. The Indian drove fast up this level valley, making the dust fly from under his car. When he came to the first house he stopped and carried packages in. Marian saw no one. In the fields, however, were picturesque labourers she took to be Indians. Upon resuming the journey her guide pointed out some low stone houses, standing back under shelving cliffs, surrounded by greening trees. These were the homes of missionaries. From that point the road ascended the side of a steep gorge. Up on top of this elevation the land was level, covered with rough low bushes, dull green in colour. Grey and red buildings showed in the distance, and long lines of bare trees. In a few moments the car had reached them. Marian was consumed with interest and curiosity.

'Mesa. We stop little while,' said the driver, coming to a halt before one of the stone structures. It was large, with few windows, and appeared rather inhospitable looking. Little ragged wild ponies wearing crude square-topped saddles stood near by with bridles down.

'Are they Indian horses?' she asked.

'Yes. Not much good. You wait,' he replied, with his reassuring smile. 'This trading post. People friendly. You go in. I take mail.'

Marian got out, glad to stretch her limbs again, and strolled to and fro. She saw a wide tree-lined avenue, with well-built grey stone houses on one side, and large red stone buildings on the other. These latter she took to be the government school quarters. How out of place they seemed! The great tableland of desert seemed to encompass them, accentuating their incongruity. The avenue was long, so that Marian could not see what lay at the upper end. Then her attention was attracted towards the trading post. A white man appeared, tall, sandy-haired, and open-faced.

'Come in. I'm Paxton, the trader,' he said. 'My wife is always glad to meet visitors. You must be tired and hungry. And it's a good way to Kaidab.'

'Thank you, I am hungry, but not tired,' replied Marian, as she followed him in, wondering how he had learned where she was going. He led her through a huge hall-like store-room, in which counters and shelves were loaded with merchandise, to another part of the house, into a living-room, comfortable and pleasant. There Marian met the trader's wife, a young and comely woman who was most kindly and agreeable. Neither by word nor by look did she manifest any curiosity. She was merely glad to meet a strange visitor and to give her a little rest and refreshment. Marian liked her.

'I'm on my way to Kaidab,' she volunteered.

'Well, I'm glad of that. It's fine of you to be interested. God knows the Indians need friends. We traders believe we are about the only friends they have.'

Marian asked casual questions about the Indians, being careful not to give an impression of more than ordinary interest. And altogether she spent a pleasant half-hour with Mrs. Paxton.

'I hope you come to Mesa again,' said her hostess, as they passed out through the store. From the door Marian saw a white man standing beside the car, in conversation with the Indian driver.

'There's Friel,' went on Mrs. Paxton, and evidently the recognition of the man changed her train of thought.

'Who's Friel?' queried Marian.

'He's a missionary,' she replied, 'but of the kind that I'm

afraid does more to antagonise the Indians against the church than to instil the true spirit of Christianity.'

Marian, somewhat startled, made no direct reply to Mrs. Paxton's statement. 'Thank you for your kindness,' she said. 'I'm sure we'll meet again. Good-bye.'

Marian walked out to the car. At her step the man designated by Mrs. Paxton turned to see her. Marian was used to meeting strangers and classifying them, after the manner of women. But she had not any recollection of a type like this man.

'I'm Mr. Friel,' he said, touching his sombrero. 'Can I do anything for you?'

'No, thank you,' replied Marian.

His face had the brown of the open, but it was not one that inspired Marian to interest or liking. Quick was she to see the gleam of curiosity in his eyes, and then, as he took a good look at her, the leap of admiration.

'You're travelling alone,' he said. 'May I know your errand?'

Marian told him what she had told the trader's wife. Then she felt rather than saw an increased interest in her, with something of antagonism.

'Have you permission to go on the reservation?' he inquired.

'No. Is it – compulsory?'

'I – well – no, hardly that. But it is always best for visitors to see Mr. Blucher.'

'Who is he?'

'The agent in charge of the reservation.'

'Very well. Where can I find him?'

'Unfortunately Mr. Blucher is away – attending an investigation. But I can take it upon myself to – to make everything all right. Wouldn't you like to see the school?'

Marian felt that perhaps she was unfairly prejudiced against the man, who was well spoken enough. But apart from that Mr. Friel had the look in his eyes which she hated. And she never met that look twice. Nevertheless, she must accept people out here in the desert as she found them, and if possible without suffering indignity, she must learn from them.

23

'It would be interesting to see the Indian children. I may return here and find some kind of work with them. But I've no time now.'

'I can get you a position here,' he said eagerly. He was too eager.

'What authority have you?' asked Marian bluntly. She omitted thanking him.

'Well, no outright authority to hire government employees,' he returned. 'But I hire people to work for me occasionally. And I'm hand in glove with Morgan. He's the power here.'

'Morgan?'

'He's been here over twenty years. And he runs things.'

'What is he?'

'Missionary.'

'So – and if I return here to find work – whom should I see first?'

'Come to me on the quiet. Then we'll see Morgan. If you got a job before seeing him you'd soon lose it.'

'Indeed! Well, I'll think it over,' returned Marian, as she stepped to the car.

Friel took hold of her arm, not to assist her, but to keep her from entering.

'Let me drive you to Kaidab. I have my car here. There's no room in this filthy junk box. Besides, a handsome girl like you oughtn't be riding alone with one of these Indians.'

'Why not? He's the mail-carrier. I'm paying him for driving me.'

'They're all alike, these Indian louts. You're not safe with any one of them.'

'If that's true, Mr. Friel, it doesn't speak well for your missionary work. I'll take a chance on this Indian. Good day.'

With that Marian resumed her seat in the car and signed the driver to start. He did so after a fashion that presupposed he was glad to leave the vicinity. Marian sat back, just as ready as she imagined he was. The breeze was pleasant. The wide coloured spaces beckoned. She was a little amazed at the heat running along and cooling out of her veins. Upon sober reflection, Marian discerned that she resented most the insult to the Indian. She turned to him.

'Did you understand what that man said?'

'I savvy him. His head big stick with skin stretched over.'

The grey clouds soon obscured the sun, and Marian again felt the chill of the wind. She bundled up once more. Her driver had turned off to the north from the Mesa road, and was following a depression of land, where Marian could not see far. There was a stretch of sandy going, then a climb up a long slope that led to a level plateau, sparsely green with plants, and monotonously grey with distance. Here the Indian put the car to its limit of speed, too fast and too noisy for Marian's pleasure.

It was only from the high places, Marian came to learn, that the incredible openness and boundlessness of the desert could be grasped. And there came a ridge summit from which she could see afar, down and across a land of prairie, on to slowly rising bare waste that swept upward to purple and black heights. These colours held her gaze. A round knob of stony hill on the left and the continuous range of mesa on her right seemed gradually to become less prominent in her sight. In another hour she learned that the black heights were forests of cedar and the purple ones were meadows of sage. Long before she reached these beautiful open patches of purple she became aware of a pervading fragrance in the air. It grew keener, stronger, sweeter. Marian recognised the odour of sage. Only how wild and strange, stifling almost, and wholly exhilarating! Here the barrenness of the desert was not in evidence. They had climbed to a high elevation. Forest of cedar and field of sage encompassed her on all sides.

If this long twenty mile upgrade of desert had not slowly grown from waste to verdure, from desolate, sinister badlands to noble heights of keen sweet air and beautiful colour, Marian would not have been prepared for the next phase of this bewildering country. But she had been given time. She had grown with the miles.

So that when the Indian driver sped his car down a steep break, round curve and corner, out of the forest into a changed world of stone, Marian was not utterly confounded. The road stretched on through a long narrow pass, above which towered cliffs of red and gold and yellow, so lofty that she had to look almost straight up to see their rims. They seemed not to be cliffs, but stone faces of mountains. Marian gazed upward until her eyes ached.

All too swiftly ran the car and all too short was that pass. It opened out upon ridged grey desert, with the black mesa on the right zigzagging away to the eastward and the red corrugated wall of stone on the left notching its bold sky-line away to the north. Ten more miles of travel removed both ramparts far to either side. And another hilltop gave Marian her first sight of Kaidab. Her letters, her gifts to Lo Blandy, had been sent to this trading post. All she saw was several low flat stone houses. A crude and dreary habitation! Yet no splendid spectacle of the whole long ride had given Marian the thrill that now shot over her.

CHAPTER 4

CLOSE at hand, Kaidab trading post showed striking aspects of life and activity. Marian looked and looked, with mounting delight and wonder.

Huge bags of burlap containing wool were being packed into a wagon by Indian freighters. And Indians were lounging around, leaning against the stone wall of the trading post. The look of them somehow satisfied Marian. Raven-black hair, impassive faces of bronze, eyes of night, lean and erect figures clad in velvet and corduroy, with glints of silver and bead ornament – these circumstances of appearance came somewhere near fitting Marian's rather sentimental anticipations.

A sturdily built, keen-eyed man stalked out of the post, with a hand on the Indian mail-carrier's shoulder. He wore a vest over a flannel shirt, but no coat or hat. His boots were rough and dusty.

'Take her bags in,' he said to the Indian.

Then, at his near approach, Marian felt herself scanned by a gaze at once piercing and kindly.

'Glad to welcome you, Miss Warner,' he said. 'Been expecting you for two hours. I'm John Withers.'

Marian offered her hand. 'Expecting me?' she queried curiously.

'News travels fast in this country,' he replied, with a smile. 'An Indian rode in two hours ago with the news you were coming.'

'But my name?' asked Marian, still curious.

'Mrs. Withers told me that and what you looked like. She'll shore be glad to see you. Come, we'll go in.'

Marian followed him into the yard beside the trading post, where somewhat in the background stood a low, squat, picturesque stone house with roof of red earth. Her curiosity had developed into wonder. She tingled a little at an implication that followed one of her conjectures. How could Mrs. Withers know what she looked like? Withers ushered her into a wonderful room that seemed to flash Indian colour and design at her. Blankets on floor and couch, baskets on mantel and wall, and a strange painted frieze of Indian figures, crude, elemental, striking – these lent the room its atmosphere. A bright fire blazed in the open stone fire-place. Books and comforts were not lacking. This room opened into a long dining-room, with the same ornamental Indian effects. And from it ran a hallway remarkable for its length and variety and colour of its decorations.

Marian's quick eye had only time for one look when a woman of slight stature and remarkable face entered.

'Welcome to Kaidab, Miss Warner,' she said warmly, with extended hands. 'We're happy to meet you. We hope you will stay long.'

'Thank you, Mrs. Withers. You're very kind. I – I am very glad to get here,' replied Marian, just a little confused and nervous.

'You've had a long, cold ride. And you're red with dust. Oh, I know that ride. I took it first twenty-five years ago, on horse-back.'

'Yes, it was hard. And cold – I nearly froze. But, oh, it was wonderful!'

Withers laughed his pleasure at her words. 'Why, that's no ride. You're just on the edge of real wild country. We're going to show you.'

'John, put Miss Warner's bags in the second room. And send some hot water. After she's comfortable and rested we can talk.'

Marian found the room quaint and strange as the others. It had a clean, earthy smell. The walls appeared to be red cement – adobe, Marian supposed – and they were cold. While washing and changing her dusty clothes she pondered over her singular impressions of Mrs. Withers. She was no ordinary woman. For some reason not apparent to Marian her hostess had a strong personal regard for her. Marian had intuitively felt this. Besides she must have been a woman used to welcoming strangers to this wild frontier. Marian sensed something of the power she had felt in women of high position, as they met their guests; only in the case of Mrs. Withers it was a simplicity of power, a strange, unconscious dignity, spiritual rather than material. But Marian lost no time in making herself comfortable or conjecturing about Mrs. Withers. She felt drawn to this woman. She divined news, strange portents, unknown possibilities, all of which hurried her back to the living-room. Mrs. Withers was there, waiting for her.

'How sweet and fair you are!' exclaimed Mrs. Withers, with an admiring glance at Marian's face. 'We don't see your kind out here. The desert is hard on blondes.'

'So I imagine,' replied Marian. 'I'll not long remain "Benow di cleash!" . . . Is that pronounced correctly?'

Mrs. Withers laughed. 'Well, I understand you. But you must say it this way . . . "Benow di cleash!" '

Her voice had some strange, low, liquid quality utterly new to Marian.

'Mrs. Withers, you know where I got that name,' asserted Marian.

'Yes, I'm happy to tell you I do,' she rejoined earnestly. Marian slowly answered to the instinct of the moment. Her hands went out to meet those offered by Mrs. Withers, and she gazed down into the strange strong face with its shadows of sorrow and thought, its eyes of penetrating and mystic power.

'Let us sit down,' continued Mrs. Withers, leading the way to the couch. 'We'll have to talk our secrets at odd moments. Somebody is always bobbing in. . . . First, I want to tell you two things – that I know will make us friends.'

'I hope so – believe so,' returned Marian, trying to hold her calm.

'Listen. All my life I've been among the Indians,' said Mrs. Withers, in her low voice. 'I loved Indians when I was a child. I've been here in this wild country for many years. It takes years of kindness and study to understand the Indian. . . . These Indians here have come to care for me. They have given me a name. They believe me – trust me. They call on me to settle disputes, to divide property left by their dead, to tell their troubles. I have learned their dreams, their religion, their prayers and legends and poetry, their medicine, the meaning of their dances. And the more I learn of them the more I love and respect them. Indians are not what they appear to most white people. They are children of nature. They have noble hearts and beautiful minds. They have criminals among them, but in much less proportion than have the white race. The song of Hiawatha is true – true for all Indians. They live in a mystic world of enchantment peopled by spirits, voices, music, whisperings of God, eternal and everlasting immortality. They are as simple as little children. They personify everything. With them all is symbolic.'

Mrs. Withers paused a moment, her eloquent eyes riveted upon Marian.

'For a good many years this remote part of the Indian country was far out of the way of white men. Thus the demoralisation and degradation of the Indian were retarded, so far as this particular tribe is concerned. This Nopah tribe is the proudest, most intelligent, most numerous, and the wealthiest tribe left in the United States. So-called civilisation has not yet reached Kaidab. But it is coming. I feel the next few years will go hard with the Indian – perhaps decide his fate.'

'Oh – there seems no hope!' murmured Marian.

'There indeed seems none, if you look at it intelligently and mercilessly. But I look at this question as the Indian looks at everything. He begins his prayer, "Let all be well with me," and he ends it, "Now all is well with me." He feels – he trusts. There really is a God. If there were not I would be an infidel.

30

Life on the desert magnified all. . . . I want you to let me help you to understand the Indian. . . . For sake of your happiness?'

Marian could not voice her surprise. A tremor ran over her.

'Nophaie showed me your picture – told me about you,' went on Mrs. Withers, with an exquisite softness of voice. 'Ah! do not be shocked. It was well for him that he confided in me. . . . I met him the day he returned from the East. I remembered him. I knew him as a boy, a little shepherd who refused to leave his flock in a sandstorm. I know the place where he was born. I know the sage where he was stolen. I knew the horse-thief who stole him. I knew the woman who took him East and put him in school. . . . But Nophaie did not remember me. He went out to the sage slopes of Nothsis Ahn, and when he rode back he had not his white man's clothes, or speech, or name. He was Nophaie. And he rode here now and then. The Indians told me about him. He is a chief who wants to help them in a white man's way. But the Indians want him to be a medicine man. . . . Well, I saw his trouble, and when he came here I talked. I helped him with his own language. It returned but slowly. I saw his unhappiness. And in the end he told me about you – showed me your picture – confessed his love.'

Marian covered her burning face with trembling hands. She did not mind this good woman knowing her secret, but the truth spoken out, the potent words, the inevitable fact of it being no dream shocked her, stormed her heart. Nophaie loved her. He had confessed it to this noble friend of the Indians.

'Marian, do not be ashamed of Nophaie's love,' went on Mrs. Withers appealingly. 'No one else knows. John suspects, but is not sure. I understand you – feel with you . . . and I know more. You'd not be here if you did not love Nophaie!'

'Of – course I love – him,' said Marian unsteadily, as she uncovered her face. 'You misunderstand. I'm not ashamed. . . . It's just the shock of hearing – knowing – the suddenness of your disclosure.'

31

'You mustn't mind me – and my knowing all,' returned the woman. 'This is the desert. You are among primitive peoples. There's nothing complex out here. Your sophistication will fall from you like dead scales.'

Gathering courage, and moved by an intense and perfect assurance of sympathy, Marian briefly told Mrs. Withers of her romance with Nophaie, and then of her condition in life and her resolve to have her fling at freedom, to live awhile in the West and in helping the Indians perhaps find something of happiness.

'Ah! You will grieve, but you will also be wonderfully happy,' replied Mrs. Withers. 'As for Nophaie – you will save him. His heart was breaking. And when an Indian's heart breaks he dies. . . . I kept track of Nophaie. He had a remarkable career in college. He was a spendid student and a great athlete. I've heard that Nophaie's father was a marvellous runner. And he carried the Testing Stone of the braves the farthest for generations. . . . But what good Nophaie's education and prowess will do out here is a question. He must learn to be an Indian. Eighteen years away made him more white than red. He will never go back to the white man's life. . . . Marian, I wonder – does that worry you? Be honest with me?'

'No. I would not want him to go back,' replied Marian.

'And will you marry Nophaie?' added Mrs. Withers.

Marian uttered a little gasp. Again it was not shame that sent the prickling hot blood to her cheeks, but a liberation of emotion she had restrained. This blunt and honest woman called to her very depths.

'Nophaie is an Indian,' Mrs. Withers went on. 'But he's a man. I never saw a finer man – white or red. . . . I think you're a fortunate girl. To love and be loved – to live in this desert – to see its wildness and grandeur – to learn of it from an *Indian* – to devote your energies to a noble cause! I hope you see the truth!'

'I don't see very clearly, but I believe you,' replied Marian. 'You express something vague and deep in me – that wants to come out. . . . I ought not forget to tell you – Nophaie never asked me to – to marry him.'

'Well, it wasn't because he didn't want to, believe me,' returned the older woman. 'I've seen some lovelorn Indians in my day, but Nophaie beats them all. . . . What do you think you'll do – send for him or ride out to his home?'

'I – I'd rather meet him out – away – somewhere in the desert,' replied Marian, in thoughtful perplexity. 'But would that be – be all right? It's so unheard of – this thing I'm doing. I *want* to do it. The strongest feelings in me sanction it. But I'm sensitive – I don't want people to know. Oh, it's the cowardice and deceit of my kind.'

'Certainly it'll be all right. John will take you to meet Nophaie,' rejoined Mrs. Withers warmly. 'And no one, except John and me, will be in the secret. We'll tell the men and everyone who happens along that you've come out to work among the Indians.'

'Thank you. That will make it easier for me until I find myself. . . . I was brazen enough when I started out. But my courage seems oozing away.'

'I reckon these first days will be hard for you. But don't get blue. All will be well. You're young, healthy, strong. You have a mind. You'll have a wonderful experience out here and be the better, if not the happier for it.'

At that juncture Withers came tramping into the room.

'Say, you look like you'd be good medicine,' he said heartily, as he stood gazing, somewhat surprised and wholly delighted. 'What the desert will do to that complexion! . . . Well, miss, a Pahute Indian just rode in. He saw Nophaie this morning and talked with him. I thought you'd be glad to hear that.'

'Oh – to-day! So near!' exclaimed Marian.

'Shore can't call it near – if you mean where Nophaie is. Nigh on to a hundred miles.'

'What did he tell you?' queried Marian eagerly.

'Not much, I just asked if he'd seen Nophaie. He said he had, at sunup this morning. Nophaie was with the sheep. It's lambing time out there. Nophaie was a great shepherd boy. I've heard before how he goes with the sheep. This Pahute laughed and said, "Nophaie forgets his white mind and goes back to the days of his youth." I think all the Indians feel joy over Nophaie's renunciation of the white man's life.'

'May I take a look at this Pahute?' asked Marian.

'Come on. I'll introduce you,' replied Withers, with a laugh.

'Yes, go out with him,' interposed Mrs. Withers. 'I must see about dinner.'

'I don't want to be introduced or have this Pay – Pahute see I'm interested,' said Marian to Withers, as they passed out of the house. 'I think it's a matter of sentiment. I just want to – to look at the Indian who saw Nophaie this very day.'

'I was only joking, Miss Warner,' returned Withers seriously. 'This Pahute is a bad Indian. He's got a record, I'm sorry to say. He's killed white men and Indians both.'

'Oh! I've heard or read that fights and bloodshed were things of the past.'

'Shore you have,' said Withers, with a grim note in his voice. 'But you heard or read what's not true. Of course the frontier isn't wild and bad, as it was forty years ago, when I was a boy. Nor anything so tough as fifteen years ago when the Indians killed my brother. But this border is yet a long way from tame.'

He led Marian through the back of the grey stone house into the store.

'Here's your Pahute,' said Withers, pointing from the doorway out into the open. 'Not very pretty, is he?'

Marian peeped out from behind the trader to see a villainous-looking little Indian, black almost, round-faced, big-nosed, with the boldest, hardest look she had ever seen on a human being's face. He wore a high-crowned conical-shaped sombrero, with a wide stiff brim. It was as black as his hair and ornamented with bright beads. His garb consisted of a soiled velvet or corduroy shirt, and trousers of blue jeans. His silver-dotted belt held a heavy gun. A shiny broad silver bracelet

34

circled a sinewy wrist, from which hung a leather quirt. Altogether this Indian was not a pleasant and reassuring sight for the eyes of a city girl, new on the desert. Yet he fascinated Marian.

'Well, what do you think of him?' asked Withers, smiling.

'I'm not especially taken with him,' replied Marian, with a grimace. 'I prefer to see him at a distance. But he looks – like —'

'Like the real thing. You bet he is. But to give the devil his due, this Pahute hasn't done a mean or vicious thing since Nophaie came back. The Indians tell me Nophaie has talked good medicine to him.'

'What is this medicine?' asked Marian.

'The Indians make medicine out of flowers, roots, bark, herbs, and use it for ills the same as white people do. But medicine also means prayer, straight talk, mystic power of the medicine men of the tribe and their use of sand paintings.'

'What are they?'

'When the medicine man comes to visit a sick Indian he makes paintings on a flat rock with different coloured sands. He paints his message to the Great Spirit. These paintings are beautiful and artistic. But few white people have ever seen them. And the wonderful thing is that the use of them nearly always cures the sick Indian.'

'Then Nophaie has begun to help his people?'

'He shore has.'

'I am very glad,' said Marian softly. 'I remember he always believed he could not do any good.'

'We're glad, too. You see, Miss Warner, though we live off the Indians, we're honestly working for them.'

'The trader at Mesa said much the same, and that traders were the only friends the Indians had. Is it true?'

'We believe so. But I've known some missionaries who were honest-to-God men – who benefited the Indians.'

'Don't they *all* work for the welfare of the Indians?'

The trader gave her a keen, searching look, as if her query

was one often put to him, and which required tact in answering.

'Unfortunately they do not,' he replied bluntly. 'Reckon in every walk of life there are men who betray their calling. Naturally we don't expect that of missionaries. But in Morgan and Friel we find these exceptions. They are bad medicine. The harm they do, in many cases, is counteracted by the efforts of missionaries who work sincerely for the good of the Indian. As a matter of fact some of the missionaries don't last long out here, unless they give in to Morgan's domination.'

'Why, that seems strange!' said Marian wonderingly. 'Has this Morgan power to interfere with really good missionaries?'

'Has he?' replied Withers, with grim humour. 'I reckon. He tries to get rid of missionaries he can't rule, or, for that matter, *anybody*.'

'How in the world can he do that?' demanded Marian with spirit.

'Nobody knows, really. But we who have been long on the reservation have our ideas. Morgan's power might be politics or it might be church – or both. Shore he stands ace high with the Mission Board in the East. There's no doubt about the Mission Board being made up of earnest churchmen who seek to help and Christianise the Indians. I met one of them – the president. He would believe any criticism of Morgan to be an attack from a jealous missionary or a religious clique of another church. The *facts* never get to this mission board. That must be the cause of Morgan's power. Some day the scales will fall from their eyes and they'll dismiss him.'

'How very different – this missionary work – from what we read and hear!' murmured Marian, dreamily thinking of Nophaie's letter.

Withers explained that many of the missionaries sent out there had been misfits in other walks of life. Some of them had not been preachers. Many of them had been weak men, who found themselves far from civilisation and practically in control of a defenceless race. They yielded to temptation. They were really less to blame for evil consequences than the

36

combination of forces that had sent them out there to the bleak, wild desert. Lastly, Withers claimed that it was this system which was wrong – the system that ignorantly and arbitrarily sent inferior men to attempt to teach Christianity to Indians.

Marian sensed poignantly the subtle and complex nature of this question of the missionary work. The Paxtons had given the same impression. Again she remembered Nophaie's letter, which she had re-read only the day before, and now began to acquire her own objective impressions of what must be a tremendous issue. And suddenly she realised that she was no longer at sea in regard to her motive or intention – she had fixed and settled her determination to stay out there on the desert.

'Miss Warner, do you want me to send a message or letter to Nophaie by this Pahute?' inquired Withers. 'He'll ride out to-morrow.'

'No, I'd rather go myself,' replied Marian. 'Mrs. Withers said you'd take me. Will you be so kind?'

'I shore'll take you,' he rejoined. 'I've got some sheep out that way, and other interests. It's a long ride for a tenderfoot. How are you on a horse?'

'I've ridden some, and this last month I went to a riding-school three times a week. I'm pretty well hardened. But of course I can't really *ride*. I can learn, though.'

'It's well you broke in a little before coming West. Because these Nopah trails are rough riding, and you'll have all you can stand. When would you like to start?'

'Just as soon as you can.'

'Day after to-morrow, then. But don't set your heart on surprising Nophaie. It can't be done.'

'Why? If we tell no one?'

'Things travel ahead of you in this desert. It seems the very birds carry news. Some Indians will see us on the way, ride past us, or tell another Indian. And it'll get to Nophaie before we do.'

'What will get to Nophaie?'

'Word that trader Withers is riding west with Benow di cleash. Shore, won't that make Nophaie think?'

'He'll know,' said Marian tersely.

'Shore. And he'll ride to meet you. I'll take you over the Pahute trail. You'll be the first white person except myself to ride it. You must have nerve, girl.'

'Must I? Oh, my vaunted confidence! My foolish little vanity! Mr. Withers, I'm scared of it all – the bigness, the strangeness of this desert – of what I must do.'

'Shore you are. That's only natural. Begin right now. Use your eyes and sense. Don't worry. Take things as they come. Make up your mind to stand them. All will be well.'

CHAPTER 5

Two Indians drove the pack-mules ahead of Marian. Withers had instructed her to mount and ride after them. He would presently follow. To her disappointment, she had been given a horse instead of one of the shaggy Indian mustangs – a short, stocky horse not at all spirited and quite ugly. But when she had got astride of him, ready to try to adapt herself to saddle and motion, she found to her amaze that she did not seem to need to do anything. The horse started off. He moved briskly. But it was not a trotting gait. She had ridden at a trot yesterday, and assuredly soon tired of it. This gait was new to her, and she had imagined she knew something about horses. She felt as if she were riding in a rocking-chair that moved on a level, if such a thing were possible. The motion delighted her.

To see everything was Marian's resolve. Yet just sight of these colourfully clad Indians and the bobbing pack-mules made her forget to look anywhere else. She felt the cold puff of wind, she smelled the dust, she rode easily without any strain whatever. Then the mustangs and mules ahead suddenly went out of sight. The trail had led down over a steep bank. Presently Marian reached it. She was amazed to see a deep red gash in the earth, with crumbling walls, and a muddy, noisy stream. Mules and mustangs were edging foot by foot down a declivity right at the edge of the water. The Indians rose fast into the stream, making mud and water fly. They yelled at the mules. Marian felt her skin begin to prickle and her heart to beat unwontedly. This horse of hers manifestly had no more regard for perpendicular places than for levels. He went right down! Marian had no easy time holding on. And though not looking directly at the mules, she seemed aware of the sudden shortening of their legs. Also she heard a noise behind her.

'That's quicksand,' called Withers from above. 'Safe, but you need not hurry Buckskin.'

Marian had no time even to make up her mind. Buckskin piled off the bank and floundered into the quicksand. Marian had her first fright. She felt one of his legs go in deep, then another and another. But he kept moving. He did not let two hoofs sink at once. And once well started, he crossed that muddy stream at a sharp gait, and climbed a sandy steep trail to the top of the bank. There Marian got her foot back in the stirrup and regained some semblance of her composure before Withers reached her side.

'How do you like Buckskin?' queried he. Not a word about that awful place!

'I – I guess I like him a lot,' she replied.

'Shore thought you would. He's a pacer. You'll ride him where you'd fall off another horse. Just let him go. He knows the trail and he'll keep up. Afraid we're in for some squalls of wind.'

Withers rode ahead to the pack-mules and quickened their pace. The Indians jogged on in the lead. And Marian appeared to be left to her horse and the trail and the encompassing scenery.

Then, towards mid-afternoon, what Withers had feared and predicted came to pass. 'Sandstorm,' he said. 'But not bad. It won't last long. Get on your glasses, and cover your mouth and nose with your scarf.'

A pall of yellow swooped down out of the west. Dark and weird, magenta in hue, the sun shone through this wall of dust. The wonderful landmarks ahead were blotted out. The sweep of this desert storm seemed fierce and swift, swallowing up the monuments and the plains, and moving down upon Marian with a majestic and inevitable precision. Then it enveloped her.

Marian imagined she grew suddenly blind. And she began to choke and suffocate. She had to breathe through the scarf, which seemed a thick band and permitted no air to pass. There was not enough air. Her lungs lifted and heaved. The smell of dust seemed as stifling as the substance of it. She felt the fine, thin, stinging particles on face and neck. And when that heavy front of the storm passed by, Marian emerged just in time to escape acute distress. Riding was disagreeable still, but gradually the gusts of whirling dust lessened, until the storm blew away towards the eastward, enveloping the uplands there as it had in the west. The sun came out, most pleasantly warming Marian's cold hands and face, and lighting the desert. Soon there came the best hour of that day, close to sunset, warmer and without wind.

Withers waited for her.

'We're getting somewhere. I didn't tell you before. This is the sage flat where Nophaie used to shepherd his sheep. Here he was stolen. . . . Yonder, under that red mesa, is the place where the thieves drove his flock. We'll camp near it. Way over here – that great break in the red wall – is the pass into the Valley of Gods. Nophaie was born there.'

Marian dismounted and, gathering a bit of the fragment sage, she placed it in the pocket of her blouse, and meant to treasure it always. Then with a hand on her horse she gazed away across the plain towards the uplands where Nophaie had been born. It meant much to her, to tread on the earth that had known Nophaie's boyhood feet, to see the wild rock towers that had shadowed his birthplace. Magnificent monuments, pillars and columns and shafts, all reflecting the gold and red of the sunset, far away and infinitely lonely, speared the horizon line and the white clouds. Valley of Gods!

Marian mounted and did not look back. Her heart was full. To the fore stretched the trail, winding through the sage. It led her under the shadow of the ponderous red mesa, a massive butt with columns like an organ, standing out alone in the desert, far from the main wall of the uplands. Upon a grassy bench Withers had made camp. Already a fire was burning. The horses were rolling. The Indians were unpacking the mules.

41

'Get down and come in,' said Withers cheerily. 'Find a seat and rest yourself. We'll soon have supper.'

Marian became conscious of aching bones and tired muscles. She was glad to rest. All that pertained to this trip was of extreme interest to her, but just now seemed subservient to the personal haunting thoughts in connection with Nophaie. She forced herself to watch Withers at his camp tasks. He did not appear to be in a hurry, yet results multiplied magically, and all in a few minutes, apparently, there was supper steaming fragrantly, and a little tent stretched over a roll of blankets for her bed.

'Come and get it,' presently spoke up Withers, in his hearty voice.

'Get what?' queried Marian.

'That speech is the Western call to eat.'

Next moment she was sitting close-legged before a strip of canvas upon which Withers spread the repast. The odour that assailed her suddenly awakened a ravishing hunger. And Marian began her first meal out on the desert, with an appreciation and relish never before experienced in her life. Withers served her, then the Indians, who stood by with eager eyes, and then himself. Marian's acute senses fixed the reality of that hour – the picturesque Indians, the Western trader, forceful and wholesome and kindly, the fragrance of bacon and coffee and hot biscuits, the penetrating cold wind that swept in and blew the pungent smoke in her face, the pleasant heat of the fire on her back, and outside of that camp circle the vague sage-plain environed by looming walls.

Later Marian crawled into the little tent that was so low it touched her head as she sat upon her bed and, making a pillow of sweater and coat, she wearily unlaced her boots and slipped gratefully down under the heavy woollen blankets. She tried to think some more, to realise all that had happened, to ponder and dream over the future, but at once she was claimed by sleep.

In the morning Withers called her, and when she crawled

out of the little tent it was into a wonderful grey of dawn, cold and pure, stingingly sweet with its perfume of desert, with the great mesa standing clear and sharp and black against the eastern gold of sky.

'To-day we climb out on top,' was one of the trader's droll remarks.

An hour after starting, Marian appreciated what he meant, though she was utterly at a loss to see how they could ever surmount the tremendous red wall towards which they were riding. It looked the scarred, blunt face of a mountain. The slant of broken rock that leaned against its base might be surmountable, but it did not extend far up. For the hundredth time Marian learned that what she saw at a distance was vastly different at close range.

Marks that had appeared to be scars turned out to be ledges and lines of broken cleavage and slopes of talus and masses of broken rock, through and over which it at last seemed barely possible to climb. The close approach to this lofty barrier was not without excitement for Marian. And when Withers led off the well-defined trail that kept to the lowlands, to take a dim rough trail which turned straight for the wall, she felt a deep thrill. This must be the Indian trail never travelled by white people.

'Here's our Pahute trail,' said Withers, as he dismounted. 'It heads in from cross-country. . . . I'm sorry to say you'll have to walk. Climb slow – rest often – and in bad places keep on the up side of your horse.'

The Indians were climbing on foot, leading their mustangs. The mules were bobbing the packs up a zigzag trail. Withers likewise began the ascent. Marian followed, confident and eager, with eyes roving everywhere. What struck her singularly was the fact that, though the immense ascent appeared to be perpendicular, there was really foothold upon its slope. Whenever she halted to catch her breath she gazed at the Indians. They did not rest. Nor did the mules. How wonderfully that trail had been worked out, zigzagging the first long slope, then

43

taking to ledge and crack, and then worming from side to side up a break between two craggy capes! It made Marian dizzy to look high at the rim.

Soon the sensations of warmth and breathlessness passed to those of fire and pain. A burden pressed upon her chest and her legs felt dead. She learned that to rest long was worse almost than no rest at all. For it grew too wonderfully good, if she halted more than a moment. So she staggered along and upward, panting laboriously, hot and wet, trying to avoid Buckskin and to keep from looking down into the void that had become awful. The light grew brighter over her. She heard the trader's cheery call of encouragement. How endless that last steep zigzag to the top!

'Rest a little,' said Withers, kindly. 'And then look around. We're on the rim of Nophaie's country.'

That roused Marian to a renewed interest. First she looked back at the lowlands from which she had climbed. How far below! Straight down the trail sheered, yet she had ascended it. The Valley of Gods rose prominently out of the vast stretch of desert, now visible to the eye; and the crowns of the monuments were on a level with the great wall from which Marian gazed. They belonged to the same strata of red sandstone. All that space below and between had weathered away. Worn by wind and sand and frost! The fact was plain to Marian, yet incredible. What of the ages! This land of mystery and beauty bade fair to transform her. Far away these red stone gods stood up, aloof, stupendous, and grand. She watched them for moments, and gradually her composure and strength returned.

Marian got on her horse, not without some sharp pains, and followed the trader, deeming it best to keep him in sight. The trail was dim. On that bare ground, however, Marian believed she could have followed the fresh tracks of the horses in the lead.

The bench of fragrant green forest soon led to the base of a rocky rise where Withers waited for her.

He held back now and accommodated his progress to Marian's. She felt relieved to have him near, though she did not want to talk. Withers, however, had little to say, considering time and distance. They began a long climb up over bare yellow rock, wavy, hummocky, ridgy, with hills and holes, that somehow permitted a labyrinthine travel towards the summit. Not wholly bare was it, for Marian saw dwarfed cedars growing in niches where dust and water had given growth to a seed. Half a mile this strange slope ascended, at length reaching the level of the huge abutment of stone she had first noted from the rim below. She seemed now on the very summit of the uplands. Yet this was not true. There were farther and higher points to the westward. To the north the view offered wide contrast with long black ranges of mountains rising to peaks of white.

'Look back and down!' exclaimed Withers, with a ring in his voice. 'I've been here only once, yet I never could forget *that* – and never will.'

CHAPTER 6

THE sun climbed high and burned hot. A warm breeze, burdened with the sweet incense of the desert, blew in Marian's face. She rode on, losing track of time. No weariness nor pangs could deaden her enthusiasm or interest, nor that haunting and recurring surety of the growing nearness of Nophaie.

It was hunger that reminded Marian of the passing hours and discovered to her that she had ridden until noon. Five hours of steady riding! At four miles an hour, she had in all covered twenty miles. She wondered if Buckskin was tired. He paced on, steadfast and leisurely, as if distance or time or sun were nothing to him.

So Marian rode on, pondering thoughts thus evolved. All at once she looked up to see a tremendous gash in the green-forested earth ahead. Withers, on foot, was waiting for her on the brink of a chasm. Far across Marian saw the opposite rim, a red-gold, bare-faced cliff, sheering downward. She was amazed. The very earth seemed to have opened. As she rode up to Withers the chasm deepened to astonishing depths and still she could not see the bottom. The trader halted her before she got to the rim.

'Pahute Canyon,' he said. 'And it's bad medicine. You've got to walk fast. Because the horses can't go slow and I'll have to lead them. Be sure to keep me in sight, otherwise you might lose the trail.'

Marian dismounted, and handing her bridle to the trader she walked to the rim. A ghastly and naked glaring canyon yawned beneath her, tremendously wide and deep, bare of vegetation and blazing with its denuded and coloured slopes.

'White people don't get to see Pahute Canyon,' said Withers,

46

as he gazed from beside her. 'It's the wildest and most beautiful spot in the West. Reckon it'll be shore a spell before automobile tourists will drive in and out of her, eh?'

With that Withers looped the bridle of Marian's horse over the pommel, and started him down. Buckskin sent the stones cracking. Then the trader followed, leading his own horse. Marian watched him for a moment. Assuredly they had to descend rapidly or lose their equilibrium. From farther down in the depths soared up the mellow voices of the Indians, evidently calling to the mules. Cracking of rocks and sliding rattles attested to the nature of that descent far below.

Marian took one long, thrilling gaze at the opposite rim where she had been assured Nophaie might meet her. It seemed a most fitting place for this meeting so fraught with significance for her. A green-fringed red-gold canyon rim, bold and beautiful, lofty and lonely as the craig of eagles – it was indeed an outlook wherefrom the Indian might watch and wait.

Reluctantly Marian turned away from this vista of canyon beauty. She had not taken half a dozen steps before she forgot all about the scenery. She became suddenly and violently aware of the treachery of loose rocks and of the hard nature of contact with them. The first fall hurt her considerably, especially bruising her elbow; but it also hurt her vanity. She started anew, more carefully, and soon found herself wildly clutching at the air and balancing on rolling stones. This time she saved herself. But she had a good scare. Caution would not do on this trail. She had to step lightly and swiftly, to be off a loose stone before it could turn with her. There was a thrill in this descent, and she began to grow reckless. Action liberated her spirit, and the faster she progressed the less she felt fear. Down and down she zigzagged, growing out of breath. The slope of boulders sheered out, affording less precipitous descent. Stones as large as houses lay everywhere. Presently Marian ran out of this boulder zone upon red earth, still steep but affording safer and easier going. When she gazed upward, to

47

see the red rim far above, she could scarcely believe her eyes.
Little steps, but many of them made short work of distance!
It was an achievement that she felt proud of as she ruefully
rubbed her bruises. Then she ran on down the easy stages over
soft ground, soon to find Buckskin standing, bridle dragging in
the trail. Withers waited a little way ahead. Marian mounted,
then became conscious that excitement had kept her from
realising both pain and fatigue. She rode on to meet Withers.

'You're no tenderfoot,' he said, gaily.

'That's all you know,' retorted Marian. 'My feet appear to
be intact, but I assure you I have some tender *places*.'

'Get on and ride now. Don't be scared of the jump-off places
in the trail below. Just hang on.'

'Do you know, Mr. Withers, you have the most wonderful
and easy solution to these trail problems? . . . Just hang on!'

The trader laughed and turned his horse to the descent.
Marian let Buckskin have free rein. The clay slopes below
presented a strange variegated appearance and seemingly
stood on end. Red succeeded to yellow, and yellow to violet,
and that to pale chocolate. The horses slid down places so
steep that Marian could scarcely keep her seat in the saddle.
Some places Buckskin just slipped down. These always meant
a deep wash to cross, with a climb up the opposite side. Buckskin would not climb leisurely. He usually jumped the washes,
and before Marian could establish herself properly in the
saddle again he was loping up the bank. The result was morti-
fying to her, and sometimes painful and not wholly without
panic. Withers' admonition was faithfully acted upon by
Marian, though not always without frantic and violent
measures. Nevertheless, she had moments of thrill and
pleasure, intermingled with the other sensations. It seemed
she was descending into the very bowels of the earth. How
deep this canyon! Though early in the afternoon, the sun just
tipped the western wall. Marian grew extremely tired just
holding on, and was indeed glad when the last incline led down
to a sandy wash, that in turn opened out into the canyon floor.

They rode up the canyon to a break in the wall, where they turned upward. The mouth of this gorge was narrow and jagged, opening back into the mountain of rock.

Withers allowed her to ride for a long distance. A sandy bank ran under the right wall. Running water dashed over the rocks at the bottom of this gorge. Cottonwood trees, with foliage bright green and fresh, shaded part of the trail. Soon the rocks began to encroach upon that sandy strip. Marian saw the Indians above her on the left, toiling over the weathered slide.

At a crossing of the stream Withers bade her dismount. He filled her canteen. Marian found the water cold and fine, free of acrid taste, and very satisfying.

'You should drink oftener,' he said, as he watched her. 'You'll dry up in this desert. Well, shore you've a climb ahead. Go slow. Be careful. Rest often. You can't miss the trail.'

With that he started up a ledge of soft blue rock, leading Marian's horse. His own was evidently in the charge of one of the Indians.

The climb she began with forced husbanding of her strength and a restraint to her eagerness. Time enough, if she ever surmounted this frightful steep, to think of Nophaie! In spite of what Withers had said, Marian had little faith in her hopes. To-morrow perhaps she would meet Nophaie. With eyes seeking out the tracks of the horses and marks of the trail, Marian slowly lent her energies to the ascent. This trail must have been very old, she thought, judging from unmistakable ruts worn in ledges and places where avalanches and weathering slides had not covered it. At every convenient rock to sit or lean upon she rested. In half an hour she found the gorge opening wide, bowl shaped in the centre with slopes of broken rock leading up on all sides. Another half-hour apparently made little progress towards the distant rim, yet it brought her to solid rock. All below now appeared the slanted roof of this gorge, choked with the debris from the cliffs above.

More than once Marian heard the Indians and Withers working far above her. The clang of a hammer rang out with keen metallic sound. She had observed a short-handled sledge on one of the mule-packs; now she understood its use on the trail. Withers was cracking rocks to roll them, and breaking the corners of jutting cliff to permit the mules to swing by with their packs. She welcomed these periods, for she had long rests, during which she fell into dreams.

When she ascended to the points where trail work had been necessary she had all she could do to scramble up. And her hands helped as much as her feet. An endless stairway of steps in solid rock, manifold in character, with every conceivable angle and crack and sharp point and narrow ledge. Mostly she feared the narrow ledges. For if she slipped on those it might mean the end of her. Treading these, she dare not look over into the abyss, now assuming dreadful depths.

This toil took Marian not only far upward, but far back into the gorge. The sky seemed to lighten. The ragged red rim above seemed possibly attainable. Below her shadows of purple began to gather under the deep walls. Her watch told the hour of five. Marian feared she had made too leisurely a task of it, or had rested too long. Still, these had been her orders from Withers. But the long climb all alone, the persistent exertion, the holding back of emotion, the whole time increasingly fraught with suspense had begun to weaken her.

Once more the character of the slope changed. The solid gleaming granite gave way to soft red sandstone; and the long reaches of ledge and short steps to wide zigzags, the corners of which turned on promontories that sheered out over the depths. Marian found the going easier here and, if she had not been worn out she would have climbed well. As it was she dragged her weary feet, slow step after step, up the long slants of trail.

Six o'clock by her watch and the gold of sunset on the far points of the rim! It seemed only a short climb now, from every turn, yet she did not get there. Nevertheless, weary and almost desperate as she was, the moment came when the strange glamour of that canyon stole over her.

50

Slowly Marian toiled round an abrupt corner on a bare promontory. She paused, her eyes on the incredible steps she had ascended. Her breast heaved. A cold wind from above cooled her hot, uncovered brow.

Suddenly a cry startled her. Piercingly high and strange it pealed down, and the echoes from the canyon walls magnified it and clapped it from cliff to cliff, until it died weirdly far below.

With uplift of head Marian swept the rim above. An Indian stood silhouetted against the gold of sky. Slender and tall, motionless as a statue, he stood, a black figure in singular harmony with the wildness and nobility of that height.

'Nophaie!' whispered Marian, with a leap of her heart.

He waved his hand aloft, a slow gesture, significant and thrilling. Marian waved her sombrero in reply, and tried to call out, but just then her voice failed. Wheeling away with swift strides, shot through and through with a current of fire, she began the last few zigzags of that trail.

Endless that last climb – unattainable the rim! Marian had overreached herself. Dizzy, half blind, with bursting heart she went on, upward, towards Nophaie. She saw him dimly as in a dream. He was coming. How strange the light! Night already? Vaguely the rim wall waved and rocked, grew darker.

No, she had not fainted. Not for one second had she wholly lost sense of that close, hard contact, of an arm like iron around her, of being borne upward. Then – one long moment – not clear, and again she felt the bursting throb of her heart – that pang in her breast. Her breath came and went in hurried little gasps. The dimness left her eyes. She saw the gorge, a blue abyss, yawning down into the purple depths of Pahute Canyon. But she could not see anything else, for she was unable to move. Nophaie held her close, her cheek against his breast.

'Benow di cleash!'

'Nophaie!'

51

There was no other greeting between them. He did not kiss her, and his close clasp slowly loosened. Marian rallied to the extent of being able to stand and she slipped away from him, still holding his hand. The Indian she had known as Lo Blandy had changed with the resigning of that white man's name. Dark as bronze his fine face had grown, lean and older, graver, with long sloping lines of pain, not wholly hidden by his smile of welcome. His eyes, black and piercing with intense light, burned into hers. Unutterable love and joy shone in them.

'Nophaie – you have – changed,' she said breathlessly.

'So have you,' he replied. An indefinable difference in the tone of his voice struck Marian forcibly. It was lower, softer, with something liquid in its depth, something proving that his mother tongue had returned to detract from the white man's.

'Must we get acquainted all over?' she asked, seriously.

'You must.'

'Very well, I am ready.'

'Then you have come to work among my people?'

'Of course,' replied Marian simply. 'I've come to do what you want me to.'

Love and loyalty spoke unmistakably in her voice and in the gaze with which she met his piercing eyes. For an instant, then, Marian trembled in a consciousness of his gratitude, of his sudden fierce desire to gather her to his breast. She felt that, and saw it in the slight leap of his frame.

'You are noble. You prove my faith. You save me from hate of the white race.' Loosening her hands, he took a long stride towards the rim and gazed away across the purple canyon.

Then Marian had her first real sight of him. This appeared but a shadow of the magnificent form of the famous athlete, Lo Blandy. Thinned out, lean and hard he looked. He was dressed in worn corduroy and velveteen, with silver-buckled belt and brown moccasins. His black hair was drawn back and bound under a red band that encircled his head. This garb, and the wonderful poise of his lofty figure against the background of wild canyon, removed him immeasurably from the man Marian had known as Lo Blandy. If there had ever been anything untrue or unreal about him, it was gone now. He satisfied some long unknown yearning in Marian's heart. Even the suggestion of the tragic was not discordant. What was in his soul then?

'I'm glad for what you think I am,' she said, stepping to his side. 'For what you say I do . . . and I want to – to make you happy.'

'Happy! Benow di cleash, this is the first happy moment I have ever lived – since I was a shepherd boy – Nophaie, down there with the sheep. Happy, because, Indian as I am, I know you love me.'

'Yes, I – I love you, Nophaie,' she said, low, unsteadily. She wanted him to know again, at once.

Hand in hand then they gazed out across the purpling depths and the gold-rimmed walls, to the vast heave of desert beyond. The sun set while Marian watched and divined the strange exaltation of the moment. Incalculable were to be her blessings – the glory of loving, and forgetting self, the work that was to be hers, the knowledge of this lonely and beautiful land, seen through the eyes and soul of an Indian. Marian marvelled now that she had ever hesitated or feared.

Then they rode side by side through a fragrant level land of piñon and sage, with the afterglow of sunset lighting the western sky. The romance of that moment seemed an enchantment of her dreams. Here was the gloaming hour, and a beautiful place of the desert wilderness, and the man she loved.

Presently the thickening twilight was pierced by the bright blaze of a camp fire. And Marian followed the Indian down into a shallow ravine where a gleam of water reflected the blaze and the dark branches of cedar trees. Withers was busy at the supper tasks.

'Well, here you are,' he called out cheerily. 'Marian, you're a little white through your sunburn. Get down and come in. Did you climb up Pahute Canyon? Ha-ha! I kept an eye on you. . . . Nophaie, turn Buckskin loose and lend a hand here. Shore, we'll soon have this lady tenderfoot comfortable and happy.'

Marian thought she might be a good deal more comfortable, but scarcely happier. It was about all she could do to drag herself to the seat Withers made for her. The warmth that stole over her, and the languor, would have ended in sleep but for the trader's hearty call, 'Come and get it.'

'I'm afraid you'll have to bring it to me,' replied Marian. 'If I get up I'll fall down.'

After the meal Withers and Nophaie made short work of what tasks were left to do. The two Indians appeared to mingle with the encircling darkness. For a moment the low, strange notes of their voices came back to Marian, and then were heard no more. Withers erected the little tent under the piñon near the fire, and then drawled, 'Shore, I reckon that's about all.' Then, bidding Nophaie and Marian good night, he discreetly retired to his own bed under an adjoining piñon. The night silence settled down upon the camp, so lonely and sweet, so strangely full for Marian, that she was loath to break it. She watched Nophaie. In the flickering light his face seemed impassively sad, a bronze mask moulded in the mood of sorrow. From time to time he would lift his face and turn his dark gaze upon Marian. Then she thrilled, and felt a warmth of gladness wave over her.

'Will you stay with us to-night?' she asked, at last.

'No. I will ride back to my hogan,' he said.

'Is it far?'

'For you, yes. I will ride back to meet you in the morning.'

'Is your – your home at Oljato?'

'No. Oljato is down in the lowland. Some of my people live there.'

'People? You mean relatives?'

He replied in the negative, and went on to tell of his only

54

living kin. And he fell to talking of himself – how he had chosen the wildest and loneliest part of the reservation because he wanted to be far away from white people. It was a custom of the tribe for the women to own the sheep, but he had acquired a small flock. He owned a few mustangs. He was the poorest Indian he knew. He did not possess even a saddle or a gun. His means of livelihood was the selling of wools and hides, and working for some of the rich Indians in that section. He had taught them how much better corn would grow in ploughed land. He built dams to hold the spring freshets from the melting snows and thus conserve water for the long period of drought. What his tribe needed most was to learn ways that were better than theirs. But they were slow to change. They had to see results. And therefore he did not find a great deal of work which was remunerative.

It had never occurred to Marian that Nophaie might be poor. She remembered him as the famous athlete who had been highly salaried at Cape May. Yet she might have guessed it. The white people had taught him to earn money in some of their pursuits, which he had renounced.

After a long silence, which Marian yearned to break, but could not, Nophaie rose and touched her hair with his hand.

'Benow di cleash, your eyes are heavy,' he said. 'You must sleep. But I shall lie awake. I will start back with the sunrise. Good night.'

Would he bend to kiss her? She had treasured and remembered his kisses, few as they had been. But he moved away, silently, his tall form dark against the pale starlit sky, and vanished from her sight.

Long Marian sat there, fighting sleep, fighting to stay awake to think of this place and Nophaie and her love, and what must be the outcome. Fatality hovered there in the night shadow. In Nophaie's look and voice, and the condition he confessed, she had read catastrophe for the Indian. Yet Marian could not be unhappy. She divined her power to give; and that Nophaie, stoic, nailed to his Indian martyrdom, would not wholly miss the blessedness and glory of love.

Marian repaired to the little tent and its bed of blankets. How good they felt! What a wonderful relief to stretch out and lie still! Sleep soon must deaden the throbbing of pulse, the aching of muscle, the burn of cheek. But would not her thoughts of Nophaie persist even in her dreams? Shadows of branches cast by the firelight moved on the walls of her tent, weird and strange. A·low wind rose to moan in the piñons. The desert seemed to brood over her.

CHAPTER 7

UPON awakening next morning Marian realised how dearly she must pay for her horseback rides and climbs on foot. Breakfast had to be kept waiting for her, and Withers expressed both solicitude and amusement.

'I may look funny, but I don't feel funny,' complained Marian, with a rueful face. 'How will I ever live through this trip? . . . Oh-h-h! those awful trails straight down and up!'

'We'll not go back the Pahute Canyon,' replied Withers. 'Now you eat all you can and walk around some. You'll find you feel better.'

Marian was so sore and stiff that she had not the slightest faith in what he said, yet upon following his advice she found he had spoken truly. Nevertheless, when she came to mount Buckskin she had an ordeal that left her smarting with pain. There was nothing to do but endure until gradually the exercise warmed her blood and eased her pangs. Then she began again to have interest in her surroundings.

The slow heave of piñon and cedar forest reached its highest ridge after perhaps an hour of riding. The sun was then high, and it lighted an enormous country of purple sage and clumps of piñons and yellow mounds of rock, now clear to Marian's gaze. How strong the sweet scent of sage! And seemingly the whole quarter of the west swelled and bulged into a superb mountain, rising to a dome of black timber and white snow. Away to the northward rose dim, faint outline of a red-walled desert chaos.

Withers waited for her, and as she rode abreast of his position he pointed far down and across the purple plain.

'Nophaie is riding to meet us,' he said. 'Show me how good eyes you have.'

Eagerly Marian strained her gaze in the direction he was pointing, but she could not see anything that resembled a horse and rider.

'Oh, I can't see him!' she cried.

'Farther to the left. There, in line with that clay-coloured bluff under the mountain. Keep your eye close down along the sage. . . . Two moving dots, one white – one black.'

'Yes! Yes! I see those dots. But how tiny! Can they be horses?'

'Shore they can. Nophaie is riding the black and driving the white. I'll bet there's a present for you. Nophaie has one fine mustang, I've been told. But he never rode it into the post.'

'For me! You think so? That would be wonderful. Oh, will I be able to ride it?'

'Some of these Pahute ponies are well broken and gentle. I don't think Nophaie would give you anything else.'

Marian had use for her eyes from that moment on. She rode with gaze searching for the moving dots. Sometimes she lost them and had difficulty in finding them again. But gradually they grew larger and larger until they assumed the forms of horses, loping gracefully across the sage, lending wild and beautiful life to that lonely desert. The time came when she clearly saw Nophaie, and after that when she recognised him. Then she made the astonishing discovery that the white mustang had a long black mane and tail, flying in the breeze. At closer view Marian was sure she had never seen any horse so beautiful. At sight of the Indians and the mules he halted, standing on a ridge, head up, mane flying. Then Nophaie caught up with him and drove him down into the trail, where he swerved to go round the mules. He pranced and tossed his head and whistled. His hoofs rang like bells on the stones. Marian now saw that he was almost pure white, of medium build, and well set up, with black mane and tail reaching almost to the ground. These alone would have made any horse beautiful. It appeared presently that his wildness was only a spirit of youth and temper, for he evinced an inclination to

58

trot along with the other horses. Nophaie's mount, however, was a really wild creature, a black, shaggy stallion, powerfully built, but ungainly, that had a halter round his nose as well as bridle.

Nophaie's greeting to Marian was in his Indian language, the meaning of which was unmistakable. His smile and hand-clasp would have been enough to make her happy. Then, indicating the white mustang, he said, 'I've brought you one of my ponies. He's Pahute, and the gentlest and best gaited horse I've seen out here.'

'Oh, thank you, Nophaie! How beautiful he is! You are very kind indeed. . . . Gentlest, did you say? He looks as if he'd jump right over the moon.'

'He wants to run, and he's lively, but you can ride him,' replied Nophaie. 'Would you like to try him now?'

'I'd love to, but, Nophaie, I – well – it's just all I can do to stay on *this* horse at the present moment. Perhaps to-morrow I will feel up to it. . . . How far to your camp, Nophaie?'

'I never think of distance as miles. Riding at this gait, we'll get there at noon. Suppose we lope ahead. That will rest you.'

'Lope! . . . Withers says "just hang on" and now you say lope. Very well. I consign my poor aching bones to your machinations.'

A touch and word from her were all Buckskin needed. Indeed, he seemed to be both surprised and pleased. He broke into a long lope that Marian found, to her amaze, a most agreeable change of gait and altogether delightful motion. It changed everything – her sensations, the scenery, the colours and smells, the feel of the wind. Nophaie loped beside her, outside of the trail, through the sage. How sweet to Marian the cool fragrance blowing hard in her face! Her blood began to race, her nerves to tingle. Always she had loved to go fast, to be in action, to feel her own spirit and muscle in dominance of the moment. This was beyond her wildest dreams.

That ride intoxicated Marian. When at the end of three or four miles Nophaie called for her to pull Buckskin to a walk she found herself breathless, utterly reckless, and full of wild longings to race on and on, to capture this new exquisite joy just liberated, to range the desert and forget the world.

'Oh! – splendid!' she cried. 'I – never knew – what a ride – could be. . . . You must race – with me.'

'Wait till you get on your white pony to-morrow. He will run like the wind.'

They rode on across the undulating sea of purple, for awhile at a walk, talking, and then breaking again into a lope, and from that to slower progress once more. For Marian time ceased to exist.

The baa-baa of sheep suddenly pierced the air.

'My flock,' replied Nophaie, answering Marian's quick look.

'Where?' she asked eagerly.

'In the cedars there. . . . Benow di cleash, here is the home of Nophaie.'

Marian's keen eyes swept the half-circle of country indicated by Nophaie's slow impressive gesture. She saw that they had ridden down miles and miles of gentle slope, which ended in a vale marked by richer luxuriance and purple of the sage, by clumps of beautiful cedar trees, and by isolated red and yellow mounds of rock. Above loomed the great mountain, now close enough to dominate and protect. A bare rock-floored stream bed meandered through the vale, with crystal water gleaming on smooth inclines and tinkling over little falls. A column of blue smoke rose from among the cedars. Marian could smell that smoke, and it brought rushing to memory the delight she always had in burning autumn leaves. A brooding summer solitude and peace hung over this vale.

'Here I have thought of you many and many an hour, and dreamed, and tried to pray,' said Nophaie. 'We will put your tent here, and your bed here, for you must sleep in the open, unless it rains. . . . Come now, rest awhile – then you can meet Maahesenie, my relative. You will see my hogan and my sheep.'

Nophaie helped her out of the saddle, a service she welcomed, for she was very near exhaustion again; and he arranged a comfortable seat for her in the shade of the old cedar with the beautiful pool of amber water at her feet.

'Cold snow water from Nothsis Ahn, my Mountain of Light,' he said.

'Nophaie, fill my canteen,' she replied. 'Oh, how thirsty I am!'

When she had drunk deep of that pure water, so cold it had to be taken slowly, she understood another meaning of the desert.

Nophaie came to look down upon her, with something soft and glad in his dark eyes.

'Benow di cleash – to see you here, to have you come for my sake!' he exclaimed, with emotion he had not shown before.

'Nophaie, it is as good for me as for you,' replied Marian.

'That could not be,' he replied, with grave smile. 'Your soul is not in danger.'

'Nophaie!' she exclaimed.

But he offered no word in explanation of his strange speech, and, bidding her rest, he strode away, with the dog beside him. Marian was left alone. The shade was cool, making it needful to cover herself with her coat. A drowsy buzz of bees or other insects mingled with the murmuring and dreamy low song of the stream. They seemed to lull her thoughts and burden her eyelids. She fell asleep. Upon awakening, it seemed to her a long time had lapsed, for she felt wonderfully rested. But she could not have slept long. Withers and the Indians had arrived with the pack outfit and were making camp some little distance away. It was Nophaie who brought her duffle bag and roll of bedding. Withers followed, carrying tent and axe.

'Shore you look comfortable,' was the trader's greeting. 'Isn't this sage-cedar country great? I've never seen any part of the desert to equal this.'

The two men erected the tent on one side of Marian, and

spread the canvas roll with the blankets on the other.

'Young lady, you'll see the stars and get your nose nipped to-night,' observed Withers.

'Nipped? By stars – or what?' she queried.

'By frost,' he returned. Then seriously he continued: 'I love this purple sage upland. I've come here often, though not by the Pahute trail. You wouldn't dream this fine open country jumps off over here – down into the most terrible broken desert. Rocks – canyons that're impassable.'

'Yes, I would. I saw where,' replied Marian.

'Well, I'm going to ride over here some ten miles south, round the corner of the mountain where an old Pahute lives,' continued Withers. 'I buy a good deal from him, and he buys from me. He's rich and an old scoundrel. He salts his wool. Now only few Indians do that.'

'Salts his wool? What does that mean?'

'He spreads his wool out in the sun and covers it with salt. That salt draws moisture from the air and melts into the wool, making it almost twice as heavy.'

'Withers, I've persuaded Etenia not to do that any more,' spoke up Nophaie.

'You have! Well, by golly! I'm shore glad, as much for Etenia's sake as mine. I like him. He's an industrious, intelligent Indian. The blankets of his women are the best we buy. Nophaie, he's wealthy. I should think he would go shares with you in some sheep deal.'

'Yes, he would,' replied Nophaie, 'but he wanted me to marry his daughter, and when I refused he grew very angry. Said I had Indian body and white-man mind.'

'Humph! that's pretty serious,' returned Withers soberly, and, shouldering his axe, he turned towards his camp.

'Is it serious, Nophaie?' asked Marian.

'I'm afraid so – for me.'

'Why? Because you can't – can't marry or become what this Indian thinks.'

'Both. You see my position is hard. My people are proud

that I have renounced the white man. But they expect me to fall at once into their ways. I tried. I have failed in many things.'

Thought-provoking indeed were these words to Marian, and she began to get a glimpse of the problem before her.

'I'm rested now,' she said, rising. 'Take me to see your hogan and Maah – whatever you called him.'

Beyond the stream some hundred or more yards, in an open space of higher ground, stood a large beehive-shaped mound of red earth with a column of blue smoke rising from the centre of its round roof. At nearer view Marian saw that the earth had been plastered thickly over a framework of wood. The open door faced the east.

Nophaie spoke to her in his Indian tongue – something she sensed to be ceremonious and indicative of the sacredness of his act in bidding her enter. She stooped to go in. A smouldering fire occupied the centre of this habitation called a hogan, and the smoke from it seemed to float round and round, to drift at last up through the hole in the roof. This roof was a marvel of ingenuity and skill, being constructed of heavy trunks of cedars planted in the ground, and affording support for the many thick branches that formed a concave network to hold the covering of red earth. How substantial and strong this Indian edifice! Something about it impressed Marian with a significance of its long adoption by the tribe.

A few iron and stone utensils lay scattered beside the fire. A haunch of meat hung from one of the posts, and beside it on the ground lay a sack of flour, with some boxes and tins that evidently contained food supplies. Besides these there were two beds in the hogan, one on either side of the fire, close to the wall.

'Which bed is yours?' asked Marian, unable to restrain her curiosity.

'Here,' said Nophaie.

His action designated an Indian blanket and a sheepskin with woolly side uppermost. Obviously the former was

Nophaie's coverlet, and the latter was his mattress. Marian thought of the hard bed of the Spartans. So Nophaie slept there! She forced her gaze to search farther, to the end that she saw an old coat, a leather pouch studded with silver buttons, and a worn hunting knife. These then were Nophaie's possessions and this was his home. Suddenly Marian's eyes blurred and smarted. Was that because of the acrid wood smoke and the heavy pungent odour? Whatever the causes, Marian realised she could not have remained there for five minutes longer. Nor could she utter one word as to her feelings or impressions.

'I sleep out under the cedar often, but Maahesenie doesn't like that,' said Nophaie.

'Let me see your sheep,' rejoined Marian.

She did not speak, nor did Nophaie, while they were threading a way through the tall sagebrush, the long light-green, purple-tinted sprigs of which reached to her shoulder.

Soon Marian emerged from the zone of cedars into the open sage, and here her sight was charmed by a flock of sheep and goats, and many lambs. If Nophaie had only a small flock, Marian wondered what a large one would be. No less than several hundred was her calculation of their number. Most of them were white, and many were black, and some were brown. The lambs all appeared as fleecy white as wool could be. They played round Marian's feet and had no fear of her. The baaing and bleating were incessant and somehow struck pleasantly upon Marian's ear.

Then she observed another Indian, tall and gaunt, with stoop of shoulders and iron-grey hair. He folded a thin blanket round him as he walked towards her. What a record of life was his face! Years and storms of the desert!

'Maahesenie – Benow di cleash,' said Nophaie.

'How do?' returned the Indian, extending a brown hand to Marian.

She shook hands with him and greeted him, not, however, without hesitation over the pronunciation of his name.

'White girl come far?' he asked, with slow curving arm extended towards the east. His English was intelligible.

'Yes, very far,' replied Marian.

'Saddle heap hard seat – huh?' he queried, with a twinkle in his eyes.

Marian nodded and laughed her affirmation. What sharp sight these Indians had! From a distance this Maahesenie had observed in her walk the evident telltale truth of how the saddle had punished her. Moreover, besides keen eyes he also had a keen sense of humour. This old Indian was laughing at her. But when he addressed Nophaie it was with dignity and gravity, and his gestures made known to Marian the fact that he was talking about her. When he ended Nophaie led her back towards the camp.

'What did he say about me?' she asked, very curious.

'I didn't get it all. You see, my mother tongue comes back slowly to me. But I got enough to make you vain. He said, "Eyes of the sky and hair of the sun." Then something about your skin being like a sago lily.'

'Well, bless him!' explained Marian, in delighted surprise. 'And what's a sago lily?'

'Most beautiful of desert flowers. They grow in the deep canyons.'

After supper Nophaie walked with Marian, singularly thoughtful and sad. Suddenly he pointed to a distant cone-shaped mound of stone that appeared to have a monument on its summit.

'I want you to climb there with me – to-night or to-morrow,' he said.

'Take me now,' she replied. 'But why there particularly?'

'I want you to see my Marching Rocks from there – and my Mountain of Light.'

'Nophaie – you want me to climb there – just because they are beautiful?' she queried, keen to divine his unexpressed thought.

'No. But because seen from that height they give me strength.'

'Strength?' she echoed. 'For what – do you need strength now?'

He seemed to shudder and shrink, with a strange, faint vibrant convulsion not natural to him.

'To tell you my trouble!'

Nophaie's sombre gaze, and the pathos and solemnity of his voice, further augmented Marian's fears and prepared her for catastrophe. His trouble must become hers. How singular his desire for her to climb to this particular height so that he could unburden himself! Their silent walk through the sage, and slow climb up a hill of smooth, bare stone, gave Marian time to fortify herself against disaster of her hopes. She also anticipated some extraordinary spectacle from the summit of this hill. The slope was steep, and ascent difficult. Looked at from their camp, it had not appeared nearly so high as it actually was. They climbed from the eastern side, walking in long zigzag slants, and resting often. Near the summit there was a depression, the upper side of which terminated in the point of stone that supported the monument. This pyramid of rocks stood eight or ten feet high, and crude as it was it had some semblance of symmetry and dignity. It meant something more than a landmark to passing Indians.

'Who built it?' asked Marian.

'Men of my tribe,' replied Nophaie.

'What does it mean?'

'It signifies a place for prayer. Indians climb here to pray. Never unless they have something to pray for.'

'Does each Indian make his own prayer?'

'No. There are many prayers, but they are those used by our forefathers.'

'Have *you* prayed here?' asked Marian, speaking low.

'Many times,' replied Nophaie.

With that, he again took Marian by the hand and led her up the remaining few steps to the summit of this stone hill which

66

had obstructed the view.

'We will watch the sun set over the desert,' he added. 'Sunset – the fulfilment, the glory, the end of the Indian's day! . . . White people do not rise to see the breaking of the morning light. And they do not care to watch the declining sun. But for Indians these hours are rituals.'

Every moment the spectacle changed, and out over the wasteland there was chaos of light and colour. The purple shadows turned to black; the red and yellow grew less intense. Vast rays of light slanted down from the broken sunset of clouds. Marian's emotion increased with the growing transformation.

The dark walls of granite grew dusky red; the Marching Rocks moved like mammoths, mystic evidence of the ages. Distance was made clear by the lifting of haze from the canyoned shadows, by the last piercing light of the sun. It seemed that a million facets of chiselled rock caught this dying glow of sunset and reflected it, throwing the marvel of light upon the clouds. The shadows lengthened and widened and deepened. Marian's sense of colour and proportion grew magnified or dwarfed, she could not tell which. Thousands of rock ridges, facing the sun, marched down to meet it.

The air grew chill. The desert darkened. Only a disc of the sun remained, still overpowering, still master of the day. It was sinking farther. The day was nearly done. How rosy the tips of the stone hills! Then the radiant disc of white fire vanished. A golden glow on cloud and sky marked the place where the sun had gone down. The earth of naked stone seemed to gather power, to rise, to come out clear and cold, to reach for the encroaching twilight.

Marian turned to Nophaie and said: 'I have seen. I feel all you feel. . . . Now tell me your trouble.'

Nophaie rose, lifting her with him, and towered over her, his face as she had never beheld it. Mystery and grief, age and strength, came out in the bronzed lineaments; and his eyes were terrible. Marian imagined she saw the soul of the Indian.

'*I am an infidel!*' he said hoarsely.

The shock of intense surprise sustained by Marian precluded her utterance.

'I did not know this when I came back to the reservation,' Nophaie went on, as if passion-driven. 'I tried to return to the religion of my people. I prayed – trying to believe. But I cannot. . . . *I am an infidel*. . . . I cannot believe in the Indian's God – I will not believe in the white man's God.'

'Oh, Nophaie!' gasped Marian, suddenly released from stunning surprise to consternation and horror. 'Your faith – will come back.'

'Never. My white teaching killed it. The Indian's religion is best for him. This Morgan kills the Indian's simple faith in his own God – makes him an infidel – then tries to make him a Christian. It cannot be done. There is not one real Christian Indian on the reservation.'

'Why – that is terrible!' replied Marian. 'But you – Nophaie – I am distressed. Oh, do you mean you have no belief in a future life?'

'An infidel has no faith.'

'But yours will come back. It must. I will help you. Surely your religion is as good as mine. No one realises more than I the necessity of faith in God and immortality. What good could life be without them? . . . Nophaie, we must strive and pray for yours.'

'Marian, cannot you understand?' asked Nophaie, in pathetic earnestness. 'The knowledge forced upon me by white people – my developed intelligence – makes it impossible for me to believe in the Indian's religion.'

'Impossible!' echoed Marian.

A silent and impressive spreading of his hands, gesture of impotence and helplessness, fixed in Marian's mind the immutability of Nophaie's spiritual catastrophe. The certainty of it pierced her heart. Sorrow for him was succeeded by resentment and anger at the white people who had done his soul this injury. Nophaie's soul had as much right to its inheritance of ideals and faiths as any white man's. Marian could not bring herself to the point of wanting Nophaie to accept the white man's religion. If she were in his place she would not do it. But how to help him!

'Let us go down before night falls,' said Nophaie, taking her hand.

With careful little steps Marian essayed the descent of the stone hill, which in the gathering darkness was difficult. An infinite melancholy pervaded the grey, silent desert. A camp fire blazed out of the shadow of the cedars. And by the time they had reached a level twilight had enfolded the sage.

'Nophaie, listen to my plan for work among your people,' said Marian. And forthwith she briefly told him the result of her interviews with Mrs. Withers. Nophaie not only expressed approval, but also gratitude, and was particularly desirous of having her find a place at Mesa, in the school.

'You can do so much good,' he said. 'The young Indian girls will love you. And as soon as you can speak their language you will influence them against evil. They are primitive children. There's one Indian girl you must look after. She is Gekin Yashi – the Little Beauty. She is fourteen years old, and large for her age. I know her father, Do etin – the Gentleman. He is a fine old Indian. He approves of the school and likes good missionaries, but he hates Morgan, who seems to be in control at Mesa. He is too much interested in Gekin Yashi.'

'Ah! – Nophaie, I am beginning to understand a little of the Indian problem,' replied Marian.

'That is good. Now tell me, you will stay here a little? So we can ride and climb and talk?'

'Yes, I'll stay two days. Withers cannot spare more. . . . Ride? I'll race you through the sage. . . . Then I'll go back to Kaidab – then to Mesa, where I'll begin my work, for you, Nophaie. You will come to Mesa?'

'Yes. I'll ride there every week. But we must meet in secret – somewhere out in the desert, to protect you. The agent Blucher has only seen me twice, but he took instant dislike to

69

me as soon as he learned I was an educated Indian. He is bad medicine, Marian. Blucher and Morgan run the reservation and the school, not for government or Indians, but for themselves. They keep down the better influences. They dominate government employees, and either get rid of good missionaries or put obstacles in their way. You will soon see through them.'

'Then you'll come every week,' rejoined Marian gladly. 'Oh, that will be fine! And you think I must meet you secretly? I am not ashamed, Nophaie. I am proud of – of my friendship with you.'

'Blucher and Morgan must not know you meet me,' declared Nophaie. 'You could not stay there after they found out. I'll ride to Kaidab in ten days and find out from Mrs. Withers what you've done at Mesa. Then I'll write you and tell you when I'll come.'

'And how and where to meet you? I'll have my white pony, you know. I can ride out on the desert.'

'Yes,' he said simply.

With this most important matter understood, Marian once more felt a warmth and stirring along her veins, a regurgitating of that happiness which had been suddenly crushed by Nophaie's disclosure. She would be able to see him often! That was the shibboleth of her joy – the inspiration to her endeavour. Would not her love for him and faith in him somehow gladden the dark days of his martyrdom? For she considered his life no less.

The desert night settled down, cool and still, with a blackness of shadow over sage and cedar, and the velvet sky effulgent with its myriads of white stars. Marian walked beside Nophaie, hand in hand, through the sage towards the flicker of camp fire.

CHAPTER 8

THAT year the summer rains came late – just in time to save the upland country from severe drought.

Up under the brow of Nothsis Ahn these rains were cold even in August. Sometimes sleet fell, pattering on the sage, whitening the flat rocks and patches of red earth, and crusting the woolly backs of the sheep. Maahesenie, who tended the flock during Nophaie's frequent absences, was exposed to these cold rains. Indian as he was, he did not seek shelter. The rain was good, even if it was cold. And when Nophaie returned from Kaidab he found his only relative seriously ill of a malady that had grown with the years.

Tending the flock in the rain and sleeping in wet clothes had brought Maahesenie's rheumatism in more severe form. Nophaie feared that he had come home too late. Maahesenie, relieved of his responsibility, went to his bed a very sick man. At that altitude the nights were cold, and even in daylight Maahesenie's bed in the hogan was not nearly so warm as it should have been. Nophaie made a warm and comfortable bed of sheepskins and blankets, but his sick relative would not stay in it. The bed he had always been used to was what he wanted. Nophaie had brought him blankets from Kaidab. And the first Pahute who passed got these blankets in a trade for some tobacco. Nophaie undertook to instruct his sick and contrary relative.

'Maahesenie, you have what white medicine men call rheumatism. It is a disease of the blood, affecting joints and muscles, and is caused by exposure to cold and wet. You must keep very warm and dry.'

Maahesenie looked at Nophaie as at a younger man who spoke idly of things he did not understand.

'Maahesenie is victim of the Evil Spirit,' replied the Indian. 'Maahesenie thought evil thoughts. A whirlwind, travelling from right to left, which is the wrong way, struck Maahesenie when he did not know the prayer to say. And it caused his body to be twisted. Maahesenie must have medicine to straighten him. Maahesenie must smoke the medicine in a jet pipe which the medicine man carries in his medicine bag.'

Therefore Nophaie had to ride forth across the uplands to fetch a medicine man of the tribe. This old Indian accompanied Nophaie, but held no communion with him. Plain indeed was the fact that he would rather have been alone in the hogan with Maahesenie to administer to him. He gave Maahesenie the jet pipe to smoke, and when that custom had been observed he took some salt from his medicine bag, and wetting this in his mouth he mixed it with the ashes from the pipe. Then he proceeded to rub this upon Maahesenie and to massage him, meanwhile chanting what Nophaie recognised as the Wind Chant.

The medicine man's next treatment was to procure flat rocks from the stream outside, and to pour different coloured sands from his medicine bag upon these rocks. He was a wonderful artist. These manoeuvres in sand soon took the form of symmetrical figures, over which the medicine man mumbled impressive and weird incantation. This done, he brushed the sand from the rocks, and gathering his effects together he left the hogan and went on his way.

Nophaie was not amazed to see Maahesenie very much better and able to get up. Probably if he had been a young man the treatment would have made him well. But he was old, and used up, and no faith could wholly banish disease. Next day he again fell victim to ague, to the slow twisting knot of his muscles. He gave up then and in sombre and silent stoicism awaited the end. Nophaie divided his time between Maahesenie and the sheep.

One day nearly a month after Maahesenie had been stricken a Pahute rode into camp with a letter for Nophaie. The Indian had ridden from Kaidab in ten hours. Nophaie took the letter, which had been typewritten, and was without address or signature. Yet, singular at first glance as this seemed, he knew who had written it and that it was important. Rewarding the Indian courier and asking him to stay, Nophaie repaired to the solitude of his favourite cedar and spread out the letter.

'I have ridden three times to our meeting-place, once each week on the day set, and have been disappointed, and worried and distressed that you did not come.

'To-day I met Withers at the trading post and he told me Maahesenie was dying. I am very sorry, yet relieved in that I now know what has detained you. Withers said he would wait while I wrote this letter to you and take it to Kaidab and send it to you by special messenger. He is very kind and good. You may trust him in every way. So I am writing here in the trader's office, pretending the letter is for Mrs. Withers. Believe me caution is imperative. I am already deeply involved in the secret underhand workings of this dreadful place.

'Do not send me any more letters through the mail. If you cannot come to meet me – and I'll ride out every week on the day we set – do not send messages unless in care of Withers. It is not safe. My mail from the East has been opened. I doubt not that my letters home have been opened. Some of them were never received by my aunt and friends. At first I put this down to the idle curiosity and jealousy of busybodies or of the clerk in the post office. He had done me the honour to press his attentions upon me, which I didn't accept. But I know now that he is merely a tool of Blucher. No letter of importance sent East to government or missionary board would ever get by this agent, unless favourable to him and Morgan. I suspected this, and fortunately I have written nothing home except my own personal interests, mostly concerning people there.

'Two weeks ago Blucher asked me to do office work for him several hours each day after my regular duty at the school. I thought it policy to oblige him, but I insisted on one afternoon for myself, which of course is the time I am to meet you. Blucher apparently thinks well of me. I heard him arguing with Morgan. He called me a tow-headed doll and laughed at Morgan's advice to watch me. He said I minded my own business and did not hobnob with the men or gossip with the women. Then he heard me set Friel right. You remember the annoyance Friel caused me. As for Morgan, the Indians hate him. Never in a hundred years would they believe one word he preaches or says. How can a man lie to the Indians, cheat them in money deals, steal their water and land, and expect to convert them to Christianity?

'This duty in Blucher's office has been prolific of much information for me. I see, hear, and read a great deal more than my work calls for. I feel justified in this. I am out here in your interest. Blucher is German. He is deeply concerned over the war in Europe. He hates England and he hates America. I know how to serve him to my own interest. But Morgan is suspicious of everyone. He really is in control here. He boasts of having put the "steam-roller" under former superintendents of this reservation. How he has power to do this I have begun to find out. When any new government employee or missionary comes here Morgan loses no time in his peculiar politics. By his lies and persuasions he influences the newcomer to his side, and if he is successful, which he usually is, he proceeds at once to lay some kind of a trap for that person. A frame-up, you know, instigated by him and carried out by his henchmen. If he fails, then he at once takes violent hatred of this interloper and begins the same kind of cunning to have him or her ousted. He really has something he can use against Blucher. That would not be difficult for an intelligent person to find. For instance, the half-breed Noki Indian, Sam Ween, is Blucher's interpreter. Blucher pays Sam twenty dollars a month, when he pays him at all. I asked Sam. And I saw in government papers the amount appropriated by the government for Blucher's interpreter. But Morgan has something more on

Blucher than the little matter of stealing from Uncle Sam.

'All of which leads to the point of this letter. Morgan's most important emissary is Miss Herron, the matron of the Indian girls. I have won the love and trust of Gekin Yashi. She is not only the little beauty her name signifies but she is sweet and good. I have talked much with her, and though very shy and afraid she tells me her troubles. Miss Herron hates her. And my interest in Gekin Yashi has incurred Miss Herron's enmity towards me.

'Now the situation as regards Gekin Yashi is this. Morgan talks religion to her, and to us teachers he speaks of Gekin Yashi's intelligence and that he could make a Christian of her. But it seems to me Morgan's interest in Gekin Yashi is *not* only to make a Christian of her.

'Do etin, the father of Gekin Yashi, will not allow her to go to Morgan's house or chapel. There is no rule to enforce this, and both Morgan and Blucher are angry at Do etin. Morgan has influenced Blucher to have a rule enforced whereby Indian girls are compelled to go to Morgan's chapel to hear him preach. This rule, I understand, is about to go into effect. I fear it will cause trouble among the Indians.

'But the rule will come and Morgan will have his way. Gekin Yashi is so afraid of Morgan that she actually shakes when I speak of him. The only way I can see to save Gekin Yashi is for you to steal her away from this school and hide her in one of those wild canyons until Morgan forgets her. This may save Gekin Yashi, but not the next pretty little Indian girl who will be unfortunate enough to fall into a like situation. You understand, of course, that you incur risk in attempting such a plan. Risk of your life! Risk not only of jail, but of your life! Mine may be a foolish plan, for it is certain that Indians in Morgan's employ could track you wherever you hid Gekin Yashi. But I could not think of any other plan.

'This is a long letter, my friend, and Withers is waiting. My personal messages must go until I see you, which I hope indeed will be soon.'

Nophaie pondered over this letter and re-read it, only to become more sombre and thoughtful. The plan suggested by Marian had occurred to him also, and now in the light of her revelation he decided he would risk stealing Gekin Yashi from the school. But he was tied here to the bedside of his dying relative and there appeared to be every reason to hurry to Mesa. It could not be done. Maahesenie was closer to him than Gekin Yashi.

Nophaie waited, with his burdened heart growing heavier, and while shepherding the flock he resolved in mind plans to rescue Gekin Yashi and safely hide her. It would be easy to hide her from white men, but almost impossible from Indians. Yet he must try.

Maahesenie died one night while Nophaie slept. Although he had expected this, the actual fact was a shock. More of Nophaie's Indian nature came out in the presence of death. His people were all afraid of a dead man.

Nevertheless, Nophaie paid stern and strict observance to the burial custom of the tribe. Indians of his own tribe came to view Maahesenie, but left him for Nophaie to bury. The Pahutes who rode by that day halted to express their sympathy, and then rode on. Nophaie had forced upon him the fact that the Nopahs did not care to bury their dead. They shirked it whenever possible. Their burial ceremony lasted four days and they could not eat until it was over.

Nophaie had assisted at the funeral services of several of the tribe. He knew what to do, though he could not recall most of the prayers and chants.

At dawn next morning Nophaie rode out into the sage on the trail to Mesa.

Eight hours steady riding across country brought Nophaie to the crest of the great plateau from which he saw the long green lines of poplar trees that marked the location of Mesa. Far removed was this country from the sage uplands surrounding Nothsis Ahn. Bare yellow sandy desert, spotted with pale green, and ridged by lines of blue rock, swept and rolled away on the three sides open to his gaze. Heat veils rose waveringly from sand and smoke; and the creamy-white clouds rolled low along the dark horizon line.

Some wind-carved rocks of yellow marked the spot Nophaie and Marian had chosen as a rendezvous. There was cool shade, and shelter from rain or blowing sand, and a vantage point from which to watch. Marian was not there, nor did her white mustang show anywhere down the long bare slope towards the poplars. The time was about the middle of the afternoon, rather early for Marian. Therefore Nophaie composed himself to wait.

By and by his vigil was rewarded by sight of a white horse gliding out from the green and heading towards his covert. Nophaie watched Marian come. She had learned to sit a saddle like an Indian. Nophaie felt the shadows lift from his soul, the doubts from his mind. Always sight of her uplifted him. More and more she was a living proof of many things: the truth of love and loyalty – the nobility of white woman – the significance of life being worth while for any human creature – the strange consciousness of joy in resistance to evil, in a fight for others, in something nameless and hopeful, as deep and mystical as the springs of his nature. How could he be a coward while this white woman loved him and worked to help his people? She was a repudiation of all his dark doubts. To think evil was to do evil. For the hour then Nophaie knew he would be happy, and would part from her strengthened. Nothing could cheat him out of the wonder of her presence.

At last she rode into the lane between the yellow rocks, and waved a gauntleted hand to him upon the shady ledge above. Dismounting, she tied the white mustang to a knob of rock, and climbed to Nophaie's retreat. He helped her up the few steep steps, and holding her hand, he knew she would have come straight into his arms if he had held them out to her. Never before had he so yearned to enfold her, to yield to a strong shuddering need of her. But he owed her proof of her ideal of the Indian. She had once called him her noble red man. Would he let any white man be more worthy of that word?

But five weeks had changed Benow di cleash. Did the light-coloured blouse and divided skirt, instead of the usual mannish riding garb, constitute all the difference? As she talked on and on Nophaie listened, and watched her. What had become of the fair skin, so like the pearly petal of a sago lily? Her face was now golden brown, and thinner, and older, too, except when she smiled. Only the blue eyes and hair of gold now held her claim to Benow di cleash. Her form had lost something of its former fullness. The desert summer was working upon her; the hot winds were drying up her flesh. And in repose of face there was a sadness that added new beauty and strength to her. Nophaie could accept this devotion to him and his people only because he saw that she was growing to nobler womanhood. In years to come she would look back upon this time and Nophaie without regret. He had vision to see that, and it permitted him to be happy with her.

From tales of the Indian children she shifted to an account of the intrigue at Mesa which was now involving friends she had made there, a young Texan and his wife, who were in trouble, owing to the machinations of Blucher and Morgan.

Nophaie knew the Texan, whose name was Wolterson. He was a government stockman and his duties were to ride out over the ranges to instruct the Indians in the care of sheep and horses and cattle. What little Nophaie had heard from the Indians about Wolterson was all to his credit. This heightened Nophaie's interest in what Marian had to say, and he soon gathered the truth of Wolterson's case, which held something of significance for him.

Wolterson had come to the desert in search of health. He was a cattleman and received an appointment from the government to be inspector of Indian stock on the ranges adjacent to Mesa. Being a young man of fine Southern family and highly recommended, he at once incurred the dislike of the superintendent. When he asked Blucher what his duties would be that individual succinctly replied: 'Ride around', and that comprised all the directions he ever received. Morgan solicited the good offices of Wolterson through Miss Herron's overtures to Mrs. Wolterson. As soon, however, as the Woltersons discovered conditions patent to all old residents of Mesa, those overtures fell flat. Then began the insidious, underhand, undermining work against Wolterson.

'After I've gone to-day,' concluded Marian, 'I want you to ride down and see Wolterson. Then ask the Indians about him. Soon Blucher will trump up some charge against him and call an investigation. Unless Wolterson can disprove it he will be dismissed. Then we'd lose a good friend of the Indians. Wolterson has befriended Do etin. That is the real cause of Morgan's enmity.'

'And – Gekin Yashi?' asked Nophaie, in slow reluctance.

'Safe and well, still,' replied Marian, in glad eagerness. 'She is ready to run off. We contrived to get permission for her to visit her father. Wolterson is dipping Do etin's sheep and this morning Gekin Yashi rode out to the hogan. She's there now and will remain over Sunday. You can go out there at night and make your plans to meet her as she rides back alone.'

'Do etin will be glad,' said Nophaie. 'Is Wolterson in the secret?'

'Yes. He approves. But we must not let him have a hand in it.'

'I shall take Gekin Yashi to a Pahute in the Valley of Silent Walls,' rejoined Nophaie thoughtfully. 'But few Nopahs know this place. It is down under the west side of Nothsis Ahn, deep in the canyons.'

'Valley of Silent Walls,' mused Marian. Then she flashed at Nophaie. 'Will you take me there some day?'

'Yes, Benow di cleash,' replied Nophaie. 'But you run a danger.'

'Of what – whom?'

'Me!'

Marian flushed under her golden tan and her eyes searched his. Nophaie dropped his gaze, that, alighting upon her brown hand, saw it tremble and then clench at her glove.

'You – you are jesting.'

'No. I think I am telling the truth,' responded Nophaie. 'Some day the savage and civilised man in me will come to strife. My Valley of Silent Walls is the most enchanting – the wildest and most beautiful place – the loneliest in all this desert. Walls of white and red, so high you cannot see their rims – running snow water, flowers and grass and trees! . . . If I ever got you down there I might never let you go.'

'Well, you frighten me,' laughed Marian. 'I see that you still retain some of your brutal football training. . . . But if all goes well – take me there to visit Gekin Yashi. Will you?'

'Could you get away from here?'

'Nophaie, I will never be permitted to work long at Mesa,' replied Marian. 'Some day Blucher will awake to my two-faced nature. For I have certainly used woman's wits to fool him.'

'Well, then I will take you to my Valley of Silent Walls.' Marian placed her hand on Nophaie's and looked up into his face and then down, with evident restraint of emotion.

'Nophaie – Gekin Yashi loves you.'

'That child! Why, she has seen me but a few times,' protested Nophaie, painfully reminded of Do etin's proposal that he marry his daughter.

'No matter. She has seen you enough. These Indian girls mature early. Gekin Yashi is not yet fifteen, but she is a woman in feeling. I think she is very lovable and sweet. She is quite the best scholar in the school. I have spent all the time possible with her. Believe me, Morgan is not the only venomous reptile that threatens the girl. Gekin Yashi is Indian clear through, but she has sense. She likes the ways of good white women. I have taught her that when a white woman loves she holds herself sacred for the man who has won her.'

'Marian, are you thinking that the way for me to save Gekin Yashi is to marry her?' inquired Nophaie.

'It might – be,' murmured Marian tremulously, 'if – if you —'

'But I do not love her and I cannot marry her,' declared Nophaie. 'So much has white education done for me.'

After that no more was said about Gekin Yashi. Nophaie felt a great throb of pity and tenderness for this white girl. How she inspired him to mastery of self, to beat down the base and bitter! Something of gaiety and happiness came to her in the closing moments of that meeting. Then the time arrived for her to go. Lightly touching his face with her hand, she left him, to run down the declivity and mount her mustang. Once, as she was galloping away, she turned to look back and wave to him. Her hair flashed gold in the sun. Nophaie watched her out of sight, with emotion deep and strange, half grief for the fate that was his, half exaltation that, miserable and lost Indian as he was, this woman of an alien white race made him a king.

CHAPTER 9

AT the upper end of the long poplar-lined avenue that constituted the only street in Mesa, the Woltersons occupied a little stone house built by the earliest founders of the settlement. A grove of cottonwood trees surrounded a tiny reed-bordered lake where ducks swam, and swamp blackbirds and meadowlarks made melody. Here were rich, dark-green verdure and cool shade and a sweet, drowsy breath of summer, blowing in from the hot desert.

On the other side of the Wolterson house lay a garden that bordered on the spacious playground of the Indian school.

Nophaie watered his horse at the thin, swift stream that ran down from the lake through Wolterson's garden, and along the fence to the orchards. The sun was westering low and the heat of the day was dying. Down at the other end of the long avenue Nophaie espied Indians and mustangs in front of the trading post. He went into the open gate of the Wolterson place and let his horse graze on the rich grass bordering the irrigation ditch.

'Howdy, Nophaie!' drawled a slow voice. 'Shore am glad to see you.'

Nophaie returned the greeting of the Texan, speaking in his own tongue. Few white men on the reservation had ever heard him speak English. Wolterson was a young man, tall and lithe, with a fine clean-cut face, bronzed by exposure. He did not appear to be rugged. His high-heeled horseman's boots and big sombrero were as characteristically Texan as his accent.

Nophaie dropped the bridle of his horse and took a seat where Wolterson was damming up an inter-section from the irrigating ditch. He tossed a cigarette-case to Nophaie, and then went on working. Indians rode by down the avenue. A freighter's wagon, drawn by six mustangs and loaded with firewood, lumbered along, with the driver walking. Bees hummed somewhere in the foliage and the stream murmured musically.

'The Nopahs think well of you and your work,' said Nophaie presently. 'You're the first stockman they ever praised. If you are brought before an investigating committee I'll get Etenia, and Tohoniah bi dony, and several more influential chiefs to testify for you.'

'Shore that's fine, Nophaie,' declared Wolterson. 'I'm giving you a hunch, I'll need them.'

At this juncture the little Indian boys and girls began to pour out of the big red dormitory like a stream of blue gingham. Nophaie also observed that two of the school teachers were out on the grounds with the children, but did not approach near enough for Nophaie to recognise them. Then Mrs. Wolterson appeared, coming into the garden, wearing gloves and carrying a trowel. She was a striking young woman, dark as an Indian, beginning to show the effect of desert wind and heat.

'Here comes Marian with Evangeline,' she said, as if pleased.

It was then Nophaie saw Marian leading a little Indian girl towards them, and he got the impression that this meeting was not as accidental or casual as might appear to others. The two teachers were watching Marian. And Nophaie, with his sharp eyes, caught a glimpse of a woman's face in a window of a house across the avenue. This appeared a busier thoroughfare now. Indians were riding out towards the desert. Some of the older schoolboys were playing ball. Three Indian workmen passed by, carrying long shovels over their shoulders.

'Shore,' drawled Wolterson, with eyes on the avenue, 'and here comes the champion liar of the reservation.'

Nophaie saw a heavily-built young man, roughly clad, typically Western in corduroys and boots and sombrero, swinging with rider's gait up the avenue. Upon sighting the group in the garden he swerved and, tilting back his sombrero, he lounged against the gate-post. His face was brown and broad, rather coarse, with thick lips and prominent eyes, wine dark in colour.

'Howdy folks!' he said, with a slow grin. 'You ain't really workin'?'

'Howdy, Jay!' responded Wolterson. 'I don't get much time except evenings.'

'Why, you seem to have all the time there is,' returned the other dryly, with satire. 'And look who's here – the handsome Mrs. Bob. I calculate to find me a wife like her.'

This was the first time Nophaie had ever seen Jay Lord. Careless, easy, cool, with his air of devilish insouciance, this leering Westerner did not enhance Nophaie's respect for the white men. Sight of him, so palpably other than the good-natured friend his familiarity assumed, roused something latent and dormant in Nophaie.

Then Lord espied Marian, who had come up to the fence, leading the little Indian girl. Mrs. Wolterson went over to them, answering Marian's greeting. Lord doffed his sombrero and waved it low, crude in his assumption of a dignified salute, yet dauntless in his admiration.

'I reckon I'll hang round awhile,' he said, as he approached the fence and hung over it. 'Why, who's this here little girl? Aren't you an Injun?'

'I'm not,' piped up the little girl, in astonishingly good English, 'I'm Miss Evangeline Warner.'

Nophaie had heard of this three-year-old prodigy. Her Indian mother had been glad to get rid of her, yet showed great pride in Eva's fame. For some strange reason the child, who was a full-blooded Indian, had taken remarkably to the white people's language and ways, and after two years hated the very name of Indian. She was a sturdy child, with heavy, round face and black staring eyes and straggling black hair, in neither appearance nor expression any different from the other little Indian girls. Nophaie roused to a strong interest in Eva.

'No, I'm not – I'm not,' declared Eva vehemently, and she kicked at the wire fence.

'Never mind, Eva,' said Mrs. Wolterson, as she knelt down to take the little girl's hand. 'Say your go-to-bed prayer for us.'

Evangeline appeared wholly devoid of the shyness characteristic of Indian children.

> *'Now I lay me down to sleep.*
> *I pray the Lord my soul to keep.*
> *If I should die before I wake,*
> I should worry!'

Before Marian could protest or even before the men could laugh, a loud voice, of peculiar timbre, rang out from behind:

'Shut that brat's mouth!'

Nophaie knew before he wheeled that the speaker was Morgan. And he had closer view of this man than ever before.

'Come, Eva,' said Marian hurriedly and, rising, she led the child away.

'That sounded a heap like the Old Book, now didn't it?' rasped out Morgan, glaring about him.

Nophaie saw a matured man of medium height, thick-bodied, with something slack in his physical make-up. He had a smooth face, the striking features of which were pale eyes the colour of ice and a long, thin-lipped, tight-shut mouth. He had a big nose, somewhat of a reddish hue, and his complexion was an olive tan, rather than the healthy bronze peculiar to the desert. Morgan seemed not to be an outdoor man. His was a strange, strong face, with an intense cast of thought or will, a deeply lined face, especially in the furrowed, frowning brow. He was magnetic, but it seemed a magnetism of strife of mind, a dynamic energy of brain, a tremendous mental equipment. All about him breathed of intolerance.

Jay Lord was the first to answer Morgan. 'Sounds like one of them schoolmarms, to me.'

'Mr. Morgan, I'm sure Marian could never have taught Eva

that,' interposed Mrs. Wolterson. 'Why, she was shocked! So, was I.'

The missionary might not have heard her, for all the sign he gave.

'Wolterson, the agent tells me you drove Gekin Yashi home this morning.'

'Yes, sir,' replied the stockman, leaning on his shovel and slowly lifting his gaze.

'How come?' jerked out Morgan.

'Wal,' drawled the Texan, 'if you mean what did I have to do with it – Blucher gave Gekin Yashi permission to visit her father. I am dipping sheep out at Do etin's. Had to haul supplies this morning. Gekin Yashi rode on the wagon. That's all.'

'Humph! When's she coming back?'

'I don't know. She said she hoped her father would keep her home.'

When Morgan's restless glance fell upon Nophaie it became fixed. Nophaie met that glance. One of the qualities he had not absorbed from his long association with white people was their habit of dissimulation or deceit. Something emanating from this man called to the depths of Nophaie. Not the old racial hatred of red man for white foe! It was a subtle, complex instinct, born of the moment. Leisurely Nophaie rose to his tall stature, and folding his arms he gave Morgan eye for eye.

'Are you the college Indian?'

Nophaie did not feel that he was required to answer.

'Sure, he's the one,' put in Jay Lord. 'They call him Nophay or somethin' like.'

'Can't you speak English?' demanded Morgan, sharply. 'Let's hear some of your Eastern lingo.'

'I would not have to speak English very well to do it better than you,' replied Nophaie, in his low, level tones, perfectly enunciated.

'Wha-at?' blurted out Morgan.

Nophaie eyed him with inscrutable meaning and did not vouchsafe any more.

'Have you ever been to my church?' went on Morgan.

'No.'

'Well, then, I want you to come.'

'What for?' queried Nophaie.

'To hear me preach. If you speak English as well as you brag, you can carry the word of God – of Christianity – home to your heathen tribe. Teach them how to get to heaven.'

'We have no desire to go to your heaven,' returned Nophaie. 'If there really is such a paradise as you preach about, all the land there will be owned by missionaries. And the Indians would have none to grow their corn and hay.'

'You think you're smart, don't you?' snarled Morgan.

'Morgan, the most stupid Indian on this reservation is smart enough to see through you.'

'Bah! Your tribe of gut-eaters are too ignorant to see anything, let alone the white man's religion.'

'The Indian's own religion is infinitely better for him than the white man's.'

'Humph!' fumed Morgan. 'Did you learn that at college?'

'No. I learned it upon my return to my people. What is more, I learned there is not one single real Christian Indian on the reservation, and it is your own fault.'

'That's a damned lie,' shouted Morgan, growing purple in the face.

'What do you know of the Indians out there?' demanded Nophaie, pointing to the desert. 'You have never been out there in the desert.'

'I have been missionary here for over fifteen years. The Nopahs are harsh. They are slow to appreciate my work.'

'No, Mr. Morgan,' retorted Nophaie, 'you have it wrong. My tribe has been *swift* to appreciate your work. Don't try any of your religious talk on me. It is all bunk. You are not a true missionary.'

'Insolent heathen!' ejaculated Morgan, choking, so that the

thick folds of flesh on his fat neck worked up and down.

'A missionary is a *man* sent out by church to propagate religion in the faith that an alien race will be saved,' continued Nophaie. 'It is not altogether a mistaken sincerity. The churches are sincere, and most of the missionaries are noble men. The government, too, is sincere, and trusts such men as you and Blucher. That must be the reason why you have been able to hang on here so long. If *you* were a real man you might help the poor Indians like a real missionary would do. You might teach them better ways to build, cook, harvest, irrigate, shear their sheep, and store their corn. You might teach them sanitary laws. By improving their physical condition, you might raise their moral standards. You might, by example, show them how a white man works with his hands. But you do not work. Your hands, I see, are softer than Mrs. Wolterson's – if she will permit that doubtful compliment. . . . No, Mr. Morgan, you are not a builder. You are a destroyer, and not only of the Indian's faith, but of the toil and sacrifice of true missionaries of God.'

Morgan's egotism was stronger than his restraint – his outraged sovereignty could not all in a moment be silenced.

'I – I'll put you in jail,' he said, with hard expulsion of breath.

'What for? Telling the truth?' rejoined Nophaie, in lofty scorn. 'This is a free country. I am an American. An honest Indian!'

'I'll haul you up for this,' he threatened, lifting a shaking hand.

Swift as light Nophaie leaped out of his statuesque posture, so suddenly that both Morgan and Lord recoiled, as if from attack. Certain it was that Morgan's face paled.

'Haul me into court!' returned Nophaie, piercingly. 'Haul me before your investigation committee! I would like nothing better. I will have Indians there, and *real* white men to listen. . . . Do you get that, Mr. Morgan?'

But Morgan shirked an answer, and with sombre glance

sweeping away he drew Lord with him and passed out of the gate, down the avenue. Lord's voice, low and hoarse, came back on the breeze.

Thereupon Nophaie turned to Wolterson and his wife. The Texan's habitual calm appeared to have been broken.

'Shore, you gave him hell,' he said, breathing deep. 'You could have knocked him down with a feather – and me, too. . . . About the happiest few minutes I ever passed in Mesa!'

But Mrs. Wolterson appeared pale and distressed.

'Oh, he was furious!' she whispered.

'Shore, I never saw Mr. Morgan upset like that,' returned her husband with a slow grin. 'He just couldn't believe his ears. . . . Nophaie, take a hunch from a Texan. Somehow and some way Morgan will injure you. He has had to suffer an unparalleled affront before other people. Besides, he actually was afraid of you – amazed – furious – then afraid. I felt it. I've long studied this man. And I can't prove much, but I feel he is capable of anything.'

'Well, to be forearmed is half the battle,' replied Nophaie, as he turned to his horse. 'I'll not ride to Mesa any more in daylight, nor let Morgan know I'm ever here.'

In the clear, cool grey dawn Nophaie waited out on the desert for Gekin Yashi, as had been planned.

She came into sight, a slim, dark figure on a grey mustang. The sun rose, now shining upon Gekin Yashi's raven-black hair, upon the face that was like a dark flower. Two months had changed Gekin Yashi. And never had he beheld her in other than the blue gingham uniform of the government school. She wore now the velveteen and silver and beads and buckskin common to her tribe. As she reined in the little mustang beside Nophaie her dusky eyes flashed one shy, frightened, yet wondrously happy glance at him; they were dropped under dusky lashes. Her bosom heaved. Gekin Yashi could not hide her love, perhaps did not want to. Nophaie mourned in his heart his unworthiness and the futility of his life.

'Daughter of Do etin, listen,' he said. 'Nophaie is the Indian with the white man's mind. He has come back to help his people. He is Do etin's friend. He loves Gekin Yashi, but as a brother. Nophaie will never marry. . . . He will take Gekin Yashi far into the white-walled canyons, to the Pahutes, and hide her there. And always he will be her brother and try to make her as the white girl Benow di cleash, teaching her what is evil and what is good.'

Nophaie rode away with Gekin Yashi to the northward, avoiding all trails, hiding as best he could their tracks, searching the desert with keen eyes for Indian riders he wished to avoid. In three days Nophaie reached the Pahute camp under the brow of Nothsis Ahn, believing that the few Indians to whom he had trusted Gekin Yashi would keep her secret. It cost him all his sheep to engage these Pahutes in Gekin Yashi's service. They could not leave their range and go into the deep canyons for an indefinite period without being well paid for it. Nophaie had not thought of that, but he gladly gave up his flock. It was much harder to say good-bye to Gekin Yashi. 'Nophaie! Nophaie!' she called, as he rode away. But he did not look back.

CHAPTER 10

FROM the hour Nophaie gave up his sheep to the Pahutes in payment for their care of Gekin Yashi he became a nomad – a wanderer of the sage.

With responsibility removed from his life, he was no longer tied to his lonely upland home – a fact that at first seemed grievous. But he was soon to discover how his loneliness had been a kind of selfishness which had kept him aloof from his people.

A few rides from hogan to hogan showed Nophaie that his status among the Nopahs had undergone a remarkable change. Not at once did he grasp what it was to which he must attribute this welcome change. At Etenia's home, however, the subtle fact came out in the jealousy of Etenia's daughter – she and all the Nopahs had learned of his abduction of Gekin Yashi. Nophaie was much concerned over this discovery, for it augured ill for the seclusion of the Little Beauty of the tribe. Upon consulting the old Indian, he learned that the news had travelled far and wide across the ranges, from rider to rider, from hogan to hogan, from lip to lip. Soon every Nopah on the reservation would become acquainted with the great feat of Nophaie – who had stolen Gekin Yashi from Mesa. Nophaie had been born of chieftains; he was now a chief of wisdom and valour. The spirit of the Nopahs still lived. The glory and the dream were gone, but there still lived a man of the olden time, a master. Etenia swore there was not one Indian in all the tribe who would betray Gekin Yashi.

'Nophaie will marry Gekin Yashi now,' concluded Etenia, and all his enmity seemed gone. He honoured Nophaie and feasted him, and had his braves sit round the hogan fire and sing the beautiful Nopah legends of love and courage. Nophaie was powerless to correct this impression that had gone abroad. All Nopahs, and Pahutes, too, took it for granted that the Little Beauty was destined to be Nophaie's wife. All in a day, it seemed, his fame had been transformed.

Nophaie rode far to keep his next appointment with Marian at Mesa, and for the whole hour of their meeting he talked of the change that had come through his taking Gekin Yashi away from the power of the missionary. Telling her seemed to clarify the vague and strange conceptions of what had happened to him. Then her instant joy was uplifting.

'Nophaie, now your great opportunity has come,' she said, with glad and earnest eyes on his. 'You can be a power among your people. But keep secret – that their faith is not yours.'

'I will,' he replied. In just those few words she illumined the wondering, brooding subjectiveness of his mind. Whatever he was, opportunity now smiled upon him, and it seemed great. He would be listened to and followed.

'Now let me talk – for soon I must go,' said Marian.

'No one suspects you. All they know at the agency is that Gekin Yashi has disappeared. Blucher did not care. But Morgan was furious. I heard him raving. This will make bad blood between them. And Do etin will suffer. I fear for him. I think you ought to advise Do etin to move to the very farthest point on the reservation.'

'He would not go a step,' replied Nophaie.

'Then indeed I fear for him,' said Marian.

Upon reaching the upland pasture under Nothsis Ahn, Nophaie herded his horses into a band and drove them out on the Pahute trail. That night he camped down in the deep canyon with the family who lived there, finding in this remote place that his fame had arrived before him. Welcome was his in every Indian habitation. At sunrise he headed his horses up the overhanging coloured slope of earth and rock, out on the cedared flats, down into the monument country where Oljato and the range of his boyhood called with poignant sorrow and regret, and across the red-and-yellow desert to Kaidab.

'Sure I'll buy your horses,' said Withers, in reply to Nophaie's query. 'What will you take for them?'

Nophaie hesitated a moment, then named a figure.

'That's not enough,' replied Withers. 'I'll give you five more on each horse. What'll you take – cash or trade?'

Nophaie took part of the deal in new outfit for himself, which included a gun.

'Reckon you're going to do what Blucher told Wolterson – "ride around", ' said Withers, with a laugh. 'You can do some riding here for us. I'm glad you came. Mrs. Withers was about to send for you.'

Nophaie wondered what the trader's wife could want with him, unless for something in connection with Marian. Also he was curious to see if she had any knowledge of his rise to fame among the Indians through his taking Gekin Yashi from the school. Mrs. Withers was glad to see him and was eager to hear news of Marian, but she had heard nothing of his abducting Do etin's daughter.

'Nophaie, I would like you to help us here in a little job – our kind of missionary work,' she said presently. 'Do you know this half-crazy Indian we call Shoie?'

'No,' replied Nophaie.

'Well, he claimed to have bewitched a squaw who died. And he has told two other squaws that he means to work his spell upon them. The first one, Nolgoshie, the loping woman, got to thinking about this, and she fell sick. I'm afraid it will kill her. I want you to help me get Shoie to say he will remove his spell. Then ride over to Nolgoshie's hogan and tell her. The other squaw is the wife of Beleanth do de jodie. He is a rich Nopah and a good man. I'm afraid his wife will also get to brooding about this spell.'

'I can influence this Shoie,' he replied, and then briefly related what had happened in Wolterson's yard at Mesa, his

93

taking Gekin Yashi away into hiding, and the strange reaction of his tribe.

Mrs. Withers grew intensely animated, almost excited, and she seemed at the halfway point between elation and anxiety.

'So *that* was it!' she exclaimed. 'I've been wondering about this sudden interest in you. Well, Nophaie, there is no other single thing you could have done to establish a great name for yourself among the Indians. That will put you high up. So in one way it is good, for no matter what happens, your name is made. But it is bad in other ways. They will get Gekin Yashi. Some of the Nokis will trail her. If Blucher finds out your part in it he will arrest you. And when they do find Gekin Yashi I wonder how Do etin will act.'

Thereupon Nophaie told of Do etin's anger.

'That is very bad,' she said gravely. 'Do etin can't keep Gekin Yashi from going to Morgan's chapel, once that rule is put into effect. You see, the Indians are really prisoners on this reservation. They have to obey the government. If they don't they will be forced to. . . . That is bad. Do etin will never break his word or give in. It means jail for him – or worse.'

Nophaie took some time over the selection of his outfit, especially the gun. He felt himself a novice in the use of firearms, and after considerable deliberation he decided a small weapon he could conceal if desirable, or carry on his belt, would be best for him.

'Here's your man Shoie,' said Withers, coming into the post.

Shoie appeared to be an Indian of perhaps twenty years of age, a big-headed brave with bushy hair, from which he derived his name. His face might have impressed a superstitious squaw, but Nophaie saw it as that of a vain, sullen Indian, lacking in intelligence. Shoie's garb was not that of a prosperous Nopah.

He was evidently flattered to be singled out of the group of Indians, and showed the same deference for Nophaie that had become universal. Nophaie affected to be impressed with Shoie, bought cigarettes and canned fruit and cakes for him, and spent some time with him before broaching the subject of Shoie's spell of bewitchment. Then Shoie denied that he had cast a spell upon any squaw. But after some persuasion he confessed it, saying these women were possessed of evil spirits which he wanted to exorcise. Nophaie at length induced him to say that he would remove the spell.

Nophaie decided at once to ride out to the hogans of these Indians and take Shoie with him. When Mrs. Withers had been informed she asked to see Shoie, and conversed with him for a moment.

'Maybe it will work,' she said to Nophaie, 'but I have my doubts. Shoie is much impressed. He thinks he's a big fellow. He sees that he can make himself felt. Now what will happen is this. He'll do as you want to-day. But to-morrow or some other day he'll tell the Indians he has put back the spell. You see, he's just demented enough to make the superstitious Indians afraid of him.'

Nolgoshie, the loping woman, lived out across the desert, in a canyon that opened into the mountain mesa. Hogans were numerous under the looming wall of this upland. Nophaie made rather a ceremonious visit out of this trip, talking with Indians and asking some to accompany him. Nolgoshie owned many sheep. She was an expert blanket weaver. Her husband had gone off to some other part of the reservation. Nophaie found her tended by female relatives or friends. Before he entered the hogan he called these women out and told his errand, indicating Shoie, who stood by, hugely alive to his importance. The women were glad; they cast dark and fearful glances at this Indian possessor of witchcraft. Nophaie thought best not to take Shoie into the hogan with him.

Nolgoshie lay on her blankets, a squaw still young and not uncomely, and for all Nophaie could tell she looked perfectly healthy. But she was sick in her mind.

'Nophaie has brought Shoie. He is outside,' said Nophaie,

impressively. 'He will take away the spell.'

The squaw stared at Nophaie and then at her attendants, all of whom nodded vehemently and corroborated his statement. The effect on Nolgoshie was magical. Her face lost its set solemn gloom. Her eyes dilated and she sat up. Nophaie talked to her for a few moments, assuring her that the evil spirit had departed and would not return. Nolgoshie grew better even while he was there. Nophaie left, marvelling at the effect of thought upon the mind and body of a human being.

He rode with Shoie to the far end of that pastureland, some ten miles to the westwood of Kaidab. Beleanth do de jodie was at home, much concerned about his wife. She was very ill. The medicine man had done her no good. Nophaie had audience with her also, and saw at once that it was precisely the same kind of case as Nolgoshie's, only this squaw had thought herself into a more dangerous condition. Nophaie was not sure that he reached her understanding. She, at least, showed no sign of improvement. Nophaie went out to find Beleanth do de jodie pressing presents upon Shoie, an unwise proceeding, judged in the light of Mrs. Withers' words.

Next day a messenger arrived in Kaidab with news that Beleanth do de jodie's wife had died. This gave Nophaie a profound shock. He exerted himself in every possible way to keep Nolgoshie from finding out. In vain! Her own attendants, in spite of advice and importunity and threats, told her of the death of the other woman who had been under Shoie's evil spell.

Nolgoshie fell back into the panic of superstitious fears. Nophaie besought her with all the eloquence and persuasion he could command. She only grew worse. Then he galloped off in search of Shoie. At last he found him, on the very moment bragging he had put back the spell upon Beleanth do de jodie's wife, and intended to do the same for Nolgoshie.

'Come back with me,' demanded Nophaie. 'So that Nolgoshie may hear from your own lips the spell is broken.'

'No!' returned Shoie sullenly, with an uplift of his bushy head.

'You will come,' replied Nophaie sharply, and he dismounted.

The Indians present, all except Shoie, rose in respect to Nophaie. An old chief, who had evidently been listening, put his head out of a hogan.

'Nophaie is master,' he said. 'Shoie is an Indian with twisted mind. He is not a medicine man. His spell is a lie.'

Nophaie knocked Shoie down and beat him, and dragging him to his feet shoved him back to his horse.

'Get up,' he ordered.

Nophaie forced the bleeding and frightened Indian to ride with him to the hogan of Nolgoshie. But they arrived too late to lend any light to that darkened brain. Nolgoshie was raving.

Nophaie drove Shoie off with a threat to kill him if ever again he claimed to cast a spell of witchcraft on an Indian. Upon Nophaie's return to Kaidab with the news Mrs. Withers expressed sorrow, but not surprise.

'I knew just what would happen,' she added. 'Nolgoshie will die.'

And next day came the messenger with news of her death and that none of the Indians would bury her. Nophaie took this duty upon himself.

CHAPTER 11

MORGAN put some letters in a drawer of his desk and locked it.

'I've got the Old Book behind me,' he muttered, with a note of exultation in his voice.

He gathered together a number of typewritten pages, all soiled, with the dirty thumb marks of Indians at the bottom. These he placed in an envelope, sealed and addressed it, and placed it in his pocket, to give personally to the Indian mail-carrier. Morgan never entrusted his communications to the post office at Mesa.

His first visitor that morning was Jay Lord. Heavy-booted, lazy-striding, he entered familiarly without removing sombrero or cigarette, and his bold face wore a mask of a smile. His dusty garb attested to recent travel.

'Howdy, Morgan!' he said. 'I got back last night. Haven't seen Blucher yet. Reckon I wanted to see you first.'

'Did you find out anything?' queried Morgan.

'Wal, yes an' no,' returned Lord. 'I can't prove what Blucher wants. Them Pahutes are sure close-mouthed. But I've a hunch the Injun Nophay had a lot to do with Gekin Yashi's disappearance.'

'So had I that hunch,' retorted Morgan darkly. 'Blucher didn't want to send you. He doesn't care, now the girl has been brought back. But *I* care. And I want examples to be made of Do etin and whoever rode off with Gekin Yashi.'

'Reckon you'll never prove anythin' on either Do etin or Nophay,' said Lord dryly. 'You'll just have to frame them.'

'Jay Lord, I don't like your talk.'

'Wal, if you don't like it you can lump it,' drawled the other. 'I told you I was ready to work for your interests in the dark.

98

An' so I am. But don't call spades hearts to me. I've been ten years rustlin' round this reservation.'

Morgan's pale eyes studied the blunt, nonchalant Lord with that penetrating, sombre gaze of a shrewd man who trusted no one.

'Very well. We'll call spades spades,' replied Morgan succinctly. 'I need you. And you want to replace Wolterson. I'll see that Blucher puts the steam-roller under him. And I'll pay you, besides.'

'How much?' asked Lord laconically.

'What it's worth to me,' snapped Morgan. 'I don't pay men before they work.'

'Ahuh! Wal, we understand each other. An' is my hunch about Blucher correct?'

'What is that?'

'Wal, you wasn't particular clear, but I sort of got an idee you wanted more on Blucher, so you could steam-roll him when it suited you.'

Morgan deliberated. The way his hand closed tight betrayed his realisation that he was dealing with a shrewd, unscrupulous man whom he must bind and hold.

'You're no fool, Jay Lord. That's why I want to keep you here at Mesa. . . . Now tell me why you believe this Indian had something to do with Gekin Yashi's disappearance?'

'Wal, the day after she was lost I rode across the mesa,' rejoined Lord. 'I found where Gekin Yashi had rode off the trail. An' I searched round till I saw moccasin tracks in the sand, an' hoss tracks. I've been a horse-tracker all my days, an' there wasn't a wrangler in my country who could beat me. I jest got down on my knees an' made a picture in my mind of them moccasin tracks an' hoss tracks. Then I measured them. I trailed them tracks all day, till I seen they were goin' straight north. Then I came back.'

'Well, go on,' said Morgan impatiently. 'The Nokis did as well as that.'

'Sure. But it took them long to find out what I knew right

off – that they'd lose the trail when they came to the sage and the flat-rock country up towards Nothsis Ahn.'

'Yes, but if the Nokis lost that trail how did they eventually find Gekin Yashi?'

'Wal, I found *that* out this trip. Your Nokis didn't find Gekin Yashi. The Pahutes who had her brought her to the camp of the Nokis.'

'Hump! Pahutes? That is queer. Were these Pahutes afraid?'

'Not of you or Blucher,' replied Lord, with a sardonic grin. 'It came about this way. There's a half-nutty Nopah named Shoie. He's a spellbinder. He heard about these Pahutes having Gekin Yashi hid deep in the canyons. Of course all the Nopahs knew that. Wal, this nutty Injun sends word by a Pahute that he had put his spell upon Gekin Yashi to kill her. He'd already killed two Nopah women with his spell. The Pahutes are more superstitious than the Nopahs. They fetched Gekin Yashi out to the Nokis who were huntin' her.'

'Well!' ejaculated Morgan. 'And how do you connect the college Indian with this?'

'Wal, that's the funny part, hard to prove to anybody but myself,' responded Lord, scratching his head. 'While I was up in that country I found out where Nophay had lived an' buried his relation. Sure it's a wild country. But I rode across it, an' I finally found Nophay's hogan. I searched around for hoss tracks and moccasin tracks like them I had pictured in my mind. An' I found them, plain as print. I found clean-cut moccasin tracks on the grave of Nophay's relation. I recognised that track. An' on the way down here I asked a Nopah who buried Nophay's relation an' he said Nophay. . . . Now, Morgan, that's my hunch. It doesn't prove anythin', except to me. I *know* who stole Gekin Yashi away.'

'That's proof enough for me,' returned Morgan sombrely. 'Lord, you're a sharp fellow. I didn't appreciate you. We'll get along. . . . Now, don't tell Blucher this about the Indian. . . . Go now and do Blucher's bidding. Keep your eyes and ears open. And see me often.'

Morgan intercepted the mail-carrier and safely deposited the precious affidavit of his zeal in that trusty Indian's pocket.

He then wended his observant way up the shady avenue of tall poplars towards the agent's office. Morgan was light-footed. He stepped softly, though not from any instinct like the Indians. Manifold indeed were the intricacies of his habit of life. As he mounted the high porch steps he heard voices. Friel and the Warner girl! Morgan paused to listen.

'Let me alone,' wearily protested the girl.

The sound of scraping chair on the floor followed, then swift, soft steps, and a man's voice, with a quick note, rather hoarse. 'Marian, don't you know when a man loves you?'

Morgan opened the door and entered. Friel was trying to enfold Miss Warner in his arms and she was thrusting him back.

'Hah! Excuse me, young folks,' said Morgan, with severe levity. 'Am I interrupting a love scene?'

'You are not!' cried Miss Warner hotly, now jerking free of Friel. Her face was red. Her dark blue eyes blazed. Her bosom heaved. For the first time Morgan thought this blonde girl handsome. Only dark women appealed to him.

'So ho?' he ejaculated, with pretension of surprise. 'What was it I interrupted, then?'

'Mr. Morgan, you can judge for yourself,' replied the girl.

'Attack, I suppose,' interposed Morgan, as the girl paused breathless.

Friel confronted Morgan in suppressed agitation. He was a tall man, not yet beyond middle age, thin and nervous.

'See here, Morgan, you're at your old trick of framing someone,' he rasped out.

'Miss Warner, this is serious, but I acquit you of blame,' said Morgan, paying no attention to the irate Friel. 'Where is Blucher?'

'He went to the dormitory to consult Miss Herron.'

'Please go for him. Don't mention this unfortunate – affair. Leave that to me. I'll see you are not attacked again.'

When Miss Warner had gone Friel roused from his momentary angry consternation, and he fell into a fury. For a moment he was beside himself, flung his arms, tore his hair, and choked in his utterance.

'Friel, this is a serious charge,' declared Morgan.

'Trump it up! Hatch something! Frame one of your damned tricks!' exclaimed Friel, in low, hoarse passion. 'Bah! I'm on to you. How you jump at anything to further your nefarious ends! . . . I'm honestly in love with that girl. I want her to marry me. You interrupted my love-making — That and nothing more!'

'Friel, I'd like to believe what you say,' replied Morgan caustically, 'but Miss Warner's plain talk proves you're either a liar or out of your head.'

'My heavens! It was her temper, I tell you. She knows I didn't mean her any harm,' protested Friel.

'Suppose I call an investigation by the Mission Board? If Miss Warner testified to her convictions and if I told what I saw – you would be rather seriously involved, now wouldn't you?'

'Investigation!' Friel echoed slowly. 'You wouldn't call one on me?'

'I've been your friend here. I've kept you here on the reservation. This behaviour of yours is not becoming to a missionary. And your ranting at me did not sound like music to my ears. I might call an investigation by the board.'

'You *might*,' returned Friel sarcastically. 'Which means you won't just so long as I stand hand in glove with you?'

'Precisely. You remember that little irregularity of yours concerning the testimonials – the thumb prints of Indians who didn't know they were signing away their land and water right? For land you now have a patent to?'

'Yes, I remember – and most decidedly I remember the idea did not originate wholly in my brain.'

'That you cannot prove,' replied Morgan tersely. 'So I

think you'll be wise to stand on my side of the fence. Here comes Blucher. Not a word of this!'

Morgan locked the door of Blucher's private office. He did not need more than one sight of the agent's face to see that the German's twist of mind was at work.

Blucher was stocky of build, light-complexioned, broad of face, with the German look. Intolerance!

'What's the trouble?' asked Morgan, and it was certain he lowered his voice.

Blucher's grey-blue eyes dilated and suddenly appeared to gleam dancingly with little arrows of flame.

'What's *your* trouble?' he queried, with a laugh. 'You're stewed up, same as I am.'

'Don't talk so loud,' replied Morgan, with significant look and motion at the door of Miss Warner's room. 'I don't trust that girl. My Noki says he saw her at the Castle Rocks talking to our college Indian. If it's true I can see through a good deal. But I'm not so sure of that. The Noki wasn't close to them. But we're cautious now.'

'Suppose it was true?' asked Blucher, interested.

'It was that educated Nopah who stole Gekin Yashi from the school.'

Blucher vibrated to that.

'Who told you? How do you know? What —'

'Never mind how I get my facts. I know. That's enough.'

'But what *you* know doesn't satisfy me,' returned Blucher testily. 'I like Miss Warner. She's a fine girl. I can't see one fault in her. What's more, she's a great help to me. I'd miss her.'

'I'm not suggesting you give her a ride on my steam-roller,' rejoined the missionary. 'If she's valuable, get all you can out of her – until we know for sure. And meanwhile be cautious.'

'How're we going to know for sure? We've read some of her letters. But they didn't prove anything to me. I think you're

103

over-cautious.'

'Not me. Those letters of hers gave me an idea. She lived in Philadelphia and spent her summers at the seashore. She wrote of seeing baseball games there. Now, I've learned that our college graduate was one of the most famous athletes the Eastern colleges ever developed.'

'That Indian!'

'Yes, that Indian,' rejoined Morgan. 'I'm not likely to forget the sample he gave me of his education. That Nopah has brains. Well, I'm wondering if Miss Warner might have known him in the East. I'll write to my Philadelphia friend and ask him for more information, especially if this Nopah played baseball at the seashore.'

'Why not cut straight to the heart of a problem?' queried Blucher impatiently. 'You work in the dark.'

'It's never wise to show your hand.'

'Let's not waste opportunity. I'll have Miss Warner in here,' replied Blucher.

The missionary raised a warning hand, restraining the agent.

'Wait a moment.' Morgan's concentration of thought grew more intense. 'All right. Fetch her in. But let me question her. I'll take a chance.'

Blucher, unlocking the door, opened it and called, 'Miss Warner, please step here.'

She came in, quiet, composed, but a keen eye could have detected a slight constriction of her throat, a glistening dilation of the pupils of her blue eyes. Morgan assuredly saw the slight signs of agitation. He fixed his cold, icy gaze upon her face.

'Miss Warner, do you deny you're a friend of the graduate, Nophaie – that you meet him secretly?'

The girl's golden tan seemed to recede, leaving a clear pallor on cheek and brow. A quick breath escaped her. Then she flushed dark red, her eyes blazed as they had blazed at Friel, her head went up with dauntless spirit.

'Mr. Morgan, am I to understand that I am a hireling to whom you are privileged to put such personal questions?' she flashed at him, in counter query.

Morgan made a slight motion of his hand, as if for Blucher to dismiss her. Manifestly he had been answered to his satisfaction.

'*Do* you deny?' interposed Blucher.

'I would not deny any implication whatever made by Mr. Morgan,' returned the girl loftily.

'Very well. That will do,' said Blucher, waving her to the door, which he closed and locked after her.

Morgan signed him to draw a chair closer, and he whispered:

'It's more than I suspected. Your doll-face is a deep, clever woman. She meets the Indian. Maybe she's in love with him. Absolutely she's not what she seems.'

The agent stroked his chin and gazed with abject wonder and disgust at the missionary.

'Morgan, you look for rottenness in every man and woman because your mind is rotten,' he said. 'I don't believe what you think about her.'

Morgan's stout body jerked a little, as with the propelling of blood in sudden anger. And the lowering cold shadow of his eyes might have been thought-provoking to a less stolid man than Blucher.

'I usually find what I look for,' rejoined Morgan. 'Let's drop Miss Warner for the present. How about the Wolterson case?'

The agent unlocked his desk and produced letters and papers.

'Wolterson is about ready for your steam-roller,' said Blucher grimly. 'All my reports have gone through. Here's copy of a letter to Wolterson from Commissioner Salisbury, Department of the Interior at Washington.'

Blucher spread a paper covered with handwriting in lead pencil and he read:

105

Robert Wolterson
    Through Supt., Mesa Indian School.
Sir:
    Reports indicate that your services as stockman are not
satisfactory; that you lack energy and initiative; that you
boast you can make a living without work; that you are wholly
inattentive to your duties and have no interest in the welfare
of the Service; that you spend your time in idleness, loafing
around your quarters, at different traders' stores, or taking
pleasure trips; that you almost invariably remain in bed after
the other employees are at their work; that you have neglected
the agency stallions, which were in your care, to such extent
that one of them died; and that through your negligence a
young heifer recently died.
    You will be given ten days from the receipt of this letter to
show cause, if any, why you should not be transferred or dismissed from the Service. Your reply should be submitted
through the Superintendent within the time specified.
                                        Respectfully,
                                            Otto Salisbury.

    'Humph!' ejaculated Morgan. 'That's not much of a charge
against Wolterson. What was his reply through you?'
    'It's too long to read. Take this copy with you. One thing's
sure, Wolterson makes a strong case, and just about proves it.
More than that, he has bobbed up with influential friends in
Texas, one of them a Senator. The best we can expect is that
Wolterson will be transferred to some other point on the reservation.'
    'So much for him,' mused Morgan, with deep gaze into
space. 'Now we've serious business that necessitates unity.'
    'Yes, I know,' grunted Blucher, 'and I hate to get down to
it.'
    'If you don't make examples of Do etin and Nophaie your
authority on this reservation will absolutely cease,' declared
Morgan impressively. A singular force emanated from him.

He radiated strong suggestiveness of will.

'Damn that old Indian!' exclaimed Blucher, with sudden passion. His face set like that of a bulldog. 'I'll make him consent to that rule or – or —'

'You'll never make him do anything,' interrupted Morgan. 'You don't know Indians. Do etin will keep his words. He'll never consent to Gekin Yashi coming to my church.'

'I don't blame him a damn bit for that,' retorted Blucher brutally. 'But Gekin Yashi is not the point with me. Do etin has bucked me. He has opposed me. He will make me look weak to all the Indians. But how to make an example of him!'

Morgan leaned forward to whisper tensely. 'Send Rhur, the policeman, Glendon, and Naylor, at night to arrest Do etin. Do etin will refuse to consent to the new rule of the government. He will resist arrest.'

'For once we agree,' said Blucher in reply. 'And how about the college graduate?'

Swiftly Morgan snapped his fingers, but the lifted hand shook before Blucher's trained gaze.

'That educated Indian is the most dangerous man, red or white, on this reservation,' hissed Morgan. 'Leave him to me!'

'Then it's settled,' replied Blucher.

'Send your men after Do etin to-night,' added the missionary.

'Yes, the sooner the better. And that compulsory rule goes into effect right now.'

Morgan hurried across the wide avenue towards his house. He strode as a man who would be dangerous to meet on a narrow footway. Apparently all he saw was the hard-packed sand upon which he trod.

In his study sat the Indian whom he had expected – Noki, a slim, tall, very dark man with straight black hair, and eyes of piercing sharpness. This Indian's latest service to Morgan had been the bringing back of Gekin Yashi. Long had he been the missionary's spy and tool of craft.

Morgan gripped his arm and dragged him to the couch, there to force him down and loom masterfully over him. Moistening his lips, Morgan began in hoarse whisper of singular potency.

'Noki, to-night you pay your full debt to the white man of God. . . . Go to Do etin's hogan. Be there just at dark. Let the Indians see you, but not the white men who come. Watch these white men go into Do etin's hogan. Steal close and listen to what they say. Trust to the darkness. Listen to that council. Remember every word you hear. And watch – see every move. When the white men go away you hurry back to me.'

The Noki's sloe-black eyes shone with something more than comprehension. The Nokis were hereditary foes of the Nopahs.

CHAPTER 12

MORGAN stayed up until a late hour that night, expecting the Noki to return with news of what had actually happened. But the Indian did not come. Morgan grew rather towards a conviction that nothing unusual had occurred. So at midnight he put aside the Bible he had been studying and went to bed. His slumbers were not disturbed by nightmare or visitor.

Next morning, while at breakfast Morgan had a caller – the old man who had been the government farmer at Mesa for years. His short, wedge-shaped figure seemed energised by rugged vitality; his features were a record of the desert.

'Mr. Morgan, the Nokis down at Copenwashie are raisin' hell with me,' he began.

'Yes? What for? And when you address me pray do not be profane.'

'It's a dry season. All but two of the springs have failed. The Nokis haven't enough water for their alfalfa. Friel gets the water first for his land. That's what the Nokis are sore about. An' I'm sayin' they've got reason!'

'Why do you come to me? I deal with the souls of Indians, not their water rights.'

'Wal, Friel's deals are mostly with their water rights,' replied the farmer bluntly. 'Now my stand is this. The Nokis are industrious farmers. They've worked hard on that alfalfa. An' I don't want to see it burn up. Friel said what he did was none of my business. I want the Indians to have more of the water that belongs to them.'

'Belongs to them? How do you figure that?'

'The Nokis were here before either the Nopahs or the whites.'

'That's nothing. The water belongs to the government.

And Mr. Friel has a patent on land and water *from* the government. I couldn't do anything, even if I wanted to.'

'Friel has no horses suffering for hay or water. He *sells* his hay. The Indians need good hay and plenty of water. They can't send their horses out into the desert to live on soapweed and greasewood. These Nokis are freighters. They freight supplies from Flagerstown. That's how they earn their living. . . . They're not gettin' a square deal.'

'Go to Blucher,' replied Morgan.

'I just left him,' returned the farmer. 'He wasn't interested – sent me to you. I reckon he was upset by his men havin' to kill an Indian last night.'

'That so? I hadn't heard,' rejoined Morgan, with no especial interest. He might not have been aware of the grey desert eyes bent upon him.

'Wal, it was owin' to some new rulin' or other Blucher ordered,' went on the farmer. 'Do etin refused to obey, as I heered the story. When Rhur with his deputies, Glendon and Naylor, tried to arrest Do etin he fought – an' they had to kill him.'

'That was unfortunate,' said Morgan, gravely shaking his head. 'But Indians must learn to obey.'

'Mr. Morgan, would you be good enough to have Friel ease up on the water?' asked the farmer earnestly. 'He's usin' more than he needs. An' we haven't had a lot of rain at Copenwashie.'

'No. Such a request from me would imply that I shared your opinion as to Mr. Friel's wastefulness, which I don't.'

'Ah-huh!' ejaculated the government man, and abruptly turned on his heel. His heavy boots thumped on the porch. Then he was gone.

Late that day Morgan received the Noki spy in his study, the windows and blinds of which were closed. And peering down into the dark, inscrutable face of this Noki who hated Nopahs, Morgan heard a long story, told with all the singular detail of an Indian's subtle and faithful observance, a story strangely and vastly different from all the others concerning Do etin's tragic death.

It was again night, and one of those nights set for the Indian girls selected by Morgan to come to his chapel to hear him preach. This missionary had not mastered the Nopah language; he had merely been among the Indians so long that he had acquired a use of their tongue sufficiently to make his meaning clear.

He harangued at the still, dark faces. 'You must learn to obey me. Your people are too old to learn. They are heathen. Their God is no good. Their religion is no good. Your parents have no chance for heaven. They are steeped in ignorance and sin. They will burn for ever in Hell's fire.

'You must forget the songs and the legends and the prayers of your people. Indians are heathen. They must accept the white man's way, his clothes, his work, his talk, his life, and his God. Then some day the Indians will become white in heart.'

Thus the missionary preached for an hour to those still, dark faces. Then he dismissed his congregation, but at the door of the chapel he drew one Indian girl back.

'Gekin Yashi – you stay,' he said, as he held her. 'I will preach to you alone, so you can spread my word to your sisters.'

This Indian maiden did not have a still, dark face. It was pale and agitated, yet beautiful with its contour, its great dusky eyes, its red lips. She was trembling as the missionary led her back from the door. Suddenly he pushed her into a seat and towered over her, strung in all his body, obsessed with his fanaticism.

'Gekin Yashi, do you know your father is dead?' he asked, in harsh, sharp voice.

'Oh – no, sir,' the girl faltered, sinking back.

'He is. . . . He was killed last night – killed because he fought

111

the white men who went to arrest him. But it was sin that killed him. He would not obey.'

The missionary paused. Gekin Yashi's sweet and youthful face slowly changed – quivered with tears streaming from her tragic eyes – and set in a strange dull expression of fear, bewilderment, and misery. Then her dark head drooped.

'You ran off to the Pahutes,' went on the missionary. 'Who took you?'

Gekin Yashi made no answer.

'It was Nophaie. He will be shot the same as your father – unless you confess your sin – and then accept my religion. . . . Speak! Did Nophaie take you away?'

'Yes,' she whispered. 'But Gekin Yashi has not sinned. She is like the white girl Benow di cleash.'

Then the missionary thundered at her.

'Yes, you have sinned. You are all sin. Only the word can wash you clean. Bid me speak it – pray for you to Jesus Christ. . . . I will save you from the ice-pits and the fire-caves of Hell. . . . Tremble in your fear! – Fall on your knees, you daughter of heathen! . . . Hate that false nature worship! . . . Love me – the white man of God! . . . Promise to do what I tell you!'

The Indian girl lifted her face, and then her little brown hands that fluttered like leaves in a storm.

'Gekin Yashi – promises,' she breathed, almost inaudibly.

CHAPTER 13

MARIAN, while waiting for the dismissal she expected every day, worked on as if no untoward thing had happened. But in reality nothing was left for her save a morbid curiosity in the affairs of this government school and her faithful, stubborn, unquenchable desire to help the Indians.

These weeks of comparative inaction for Marian and the dearth of news from Nophaie and the apparent indifference of Blucher and Morgan to her presence as an employee of the government in no wise lulled her fears, and certainly of ultimate dismissal. The powers were intent on matters of more importance. Marian grew brooding and nervous, and was troubled by strange portents impossible to define. She felt that something was about to happen.

And one morning, when Miss Herron, her hard face pale and agitated, came running into the room where Marian was working, she felt a shock. Her intuition had prompted her aright.

The matron ran into Blucher's office, the door of which was open.

'Where's Morgan,' she asked shrilly. 'I can't – find him.'

'What's wrong?' queried Blucher, with a frown of annoyance at this intrusion or disruption of his thought.

'That college Indian – forced himself into the school room,' cried Miss Herron. 'He scared me out of – my wits. He's dragged Gekin Yashi into the hall – where he's talking to her. I heard Morgan's name – then I ran out – over to his house – to tell him. . . . Oh, that Indian looked terrible!'

'Nophaie!' ejaculated Blucher. Manifestly that Indian name conjured up swift and bewildered ideas. Blucher looked mightily concerned. When Miss Herron started to run out he detained her. 'You stay right here – and keep your mouth shut.' Then he grasped the telephone.

The shock to Marian had kept her standing just where she had been when Miss Herron entered. Shuffling, soft footsteps that she recognised as Morgan's gave her another shock. Then the missionary entered. Certain it was he did not know of the presence of Nophaie. But his glance at Marian, and then sight of Miss Herron in the next room, told him something was amiss.

'What – why are you here?' he demanded, entering the office.

'Shut up!' interrupted Blucher. 'Morgan, there's hell to pay. Your college Indian is here – with Gekin Yashi. . . . Hello! . . . Yes, this is Blucher. Where's Rhur? . . . Not there? Where is he? Find him quick.'

Blucher slammed down the receiver of the telephone and glared at Morgan. Marian could only partially see the missionary's face, and what she saw was pale.

'Morgan, that Indian is with Gekin Yashi now,' said the agent hoarsely. 'Your friend Herron here heard him speak your name.'

'Lock the door,' shouted Morgan, wheeling. He banged it hard. Marian heard the key turn.

Marian had a glimpse of his face as he shut the door and somehow sight of it roused her. She peered through the open door, out into the yard, towards the dormitory. A tall Indian was running fleetly towards the office. Before she could draw another breath he had reached the porch steps to mount them in one pantherish bound. His moccasined feet padded on the floor. Then – he flashed in upon her, somehow terrible. A soiled handkerchief, folded narrow, and spotted with blood now dry, circled his brow and black hair. His eyes seemed to pierce Marian.

'I saw Morgan come in,' he said. 'Is he there – with Blucher?'

114

'Oh – yes,' gasped Marian. 'They're locked in. You mustn't. . . . Oh!'

Nophaie pulled a gun from somewhere, and lunging at the locked door, he shoved his foot against it with tremendous force. The lock broke. The door swung in. Nophaie bounded across the threshold.

Marian, suddenly galvanised into action, ran after him.

Miss Herron lay on the floor in a faint. Blucher sat back in his chair, mouth agape, eyes wide. Amaze had begun to give way to fear. Morgan was ghastly.

Nophaie, with his right hand, held the gun low. It was cocked and it had an almost imperceptible quiver. With left hand Nophaie significantly touched the bloody bandage round his head.

'Do etin's murderers did not give me that,' said Nophaie. 'They came three times to find me. But they failed. It was your Noki who ambushed my trail and shot me. . . . I have his confession.'

Neither of the accused could utter a word. The Indian's menace was unmistakable, as inevitable, as it was terrible.

'Morgan – I thought well to get Gekin Yashi's confession also – so I can kill you without the compunction white education fostered in me.'

Morgan gasped and sagged against the wall. Blucher, livid and fearful, began to stammer incoherently.

'I am going to kill you both,' said Nophaie.

With that Marian shut the door behind her. Then she got between Nophaie and the men, facing them. She realised what she had to do, and was equal to it.

'Keep quiet,' she ordered.

Wheeling to Nophaie, she went closer to him, with one hand going to his shoulder, the other forcing down the levelled gun.

'You must not kill these men.'

'Why not? Blucher had his men murder Do etin. Morgan has murdered Gekin Yashi's soul.'

'That may be true,' responded Marian. 'It's not a question

115

of justice. If you shoot them you will go to the gallows.'

'Yes, if I were caught. And then I would like to tell in a court-room what these men are.'

'Nophaie, you would not be believed except by a few who could not help you.'

'Then I'll kill them in revenge. For Gekin Yashi – for my people.'

'No! No! You are above that, too. It's only your passion. There is no *good* to be accomplished. The evil these men have done will earn its punishment. Don't kill them.'

'I must. There is no justice. Your government is not honest or fair with the Indian. It never was and never *will* be. Not to save the Indian! These reservations are not for Indians. They are desert fields, isolated wastes with which a few white men induce the government to appropriate fifteen million dollars – that they may keep their fat, useless jobs. . . . The whites have educated me. And all I know cries out to kill these devils. I must do it.'

'But you are the man I love,' cried Marian, driven to desperation by his cold truth, by the remorselessness of his just wrath. 'You are the *man*. It would break my heart if you became a murderer – a fugitive from justice – and if – if they hanged you – I'd die! . . . My God! Nophaie, for sake of my love – for me – let these men live. Think of what it means to me. I'll marry you. I'll live with you. I'll spend my life helping your people – if – if only you – will not – spill blood.'

She embraced him, clung to him, weakening at the end of her long appeal.

Nophaie slowly let down the hammer of his gun. 'Benow di cleash, hold this for me,' he said.

Then with swift violence he turned upon Morgan, and in one singular powerful motion, in which his whole body appeared to participate, he shot his knee up into the man's prominent abdomen. The blow made a sodden sound not unlike a heavy beat upon a drum. Morgan crashed against the wall, his head struck hard, his mouth spread wide, and a

116

tremendous expulsion of breath followed. All the wind had been kicked out of him. As he sank to his knees his face grew hideous. His hands beat the air!

Next, in one bound Nophaie leaped upon the desk, and from that right down on Blucher, breaking the chair and sending the agent hard to the floor. Nophaie did not even lose his balance. Every time the German got to hands and knees Nophaie would swing a moccasined foot. He kicked and he shoved. And then it appeared he was plunging Blucher nearer and nearer to Morgan, whose convulsions had evidently gained him some breath. Another kick sent the agent hard against the kneeling missionary, knocking him over.

'At college I learned a great many white men's tricks,' said Nophaie, with grim humour. 'And one of them was to kick. College men claimed I could kick a football harder and farther than any other athlete who ever lived. Now since I scorn to soil my heathen red hands on such dirty beasts as you I must resort to kicking.'

And without particular violence or rancour, he kept up this game of football until both men were dishevelled bloody-nosed wretches. Suddenly he ceased. Marian saw then that Miss Herron had revived and was sitting up. Nophaie looked at her with the same disgust that the men had inspired in him.

'I ought to kick you, too,' he said. 'But I have a white man's education.' Drawing Marian out of the room, he closed the door and took his gun from her shaking hands.

'Don't be frightened, Benow di cleash,' he said, with a strong, tender arm round her. 'You saved me again. I can do nothing but love you more – and go back to my canyons. . . . Don't worry about what Blucher and Morgan will do. They are cowards. They will not speak one word of this. If you get dismissed, go to the trader's house. I beg of you – stay on the reservation yet awhile. Send me word through Withers. Good-bye.'

'Oh, Nophaie!' cried Marian, trying to find her voice.

CHAPTER 14

DEEP in the canyoned recesses of the rock-ribbed earth, far
beneath the white dome of Nothsis Ahn, Nophaie established
his refuge in one of the almost inaccessible niches of his
Canyon of Silent Walls.

He had packed supplies in from Kaidab and had left the
post with an arrangement whereby any letters from Marian
and more supplies would be sent once a month by a trusted
Pahute.

Nophaie had reasoned that if there was anything to help him
now in his extremity it was communion with his soul, and
mastery of his physical self, here in the shadow of these lonely,
silent walls.

Days passed into weeks and time was naught. The north
wind roared on Nothsis Ahn and storm clouds lodged there,
black, with dropping grey veils. But down in the Canyon of
Silent Walls there was neither winter cold nor wind. Nophaie
sought the sunny walls and dreamed in their reflected heat.
Only one arm of the canyon still remained unexplored, and he
had left that for some task of energy and action to fall back
upon when his spirit ebbed low.

One day, from far down the canyon, pealed and echoed the
call of an Indian. It startled Nophaie. He had forgotten the
Pahute whom Withers was to send with supplies. He had
forgotten that and more.

Nophaie found the Pahute in the main arm of the canyon.
He had brought a pack-mule heavily laden. Nophaie led him
to his camp, and there unpacked the mule, and cooked a meal
for the Indian, and learned from him that white policemen had
sought him all over the reservation and had returned to Mesa.
No other news had the Pahute, except that the trader at Kaidab

had told him to get to Nophaie on this day. 'Jesus Christ Day,' added the Indian with a grin.

'Christmas!' exclaimed Nophaie, and strange indeed were his memories.

The Pahute left early in the afternoon, saying he wanted to get over the Marching Rocks before nightfall. Nophaie was again alone. Yet how different the loneliness now! There were packets and packages in that pile of supplies which, despite their outside wrappings of burlap and paper, did not bear the hallmark of an Indian trader. Nophaie felt rich. It struck him significantly that he was unutterably glad. But was it not a certainty of messages from Marian? That assuredly, yet he could not be sure it was all! Unpacking the heavier parcels first, Nophaie found that the trader had added considerably to the monthly order. Then there was a bundle of lighter weight, more carefully packed, and inside was a tag upon which was written in English, 'Merry Christmas from Withers' outfit.'

Nophaie tried to be annoyed at this, but he could not, and he found that what irritated him was the happy greeting in English. 'I am an Indian,' muttered Nophaie. Yet he did not speak that in the Indian language. 'Christmas gifts and greetings,' he added, 'and I am glad.' Indian or not he could not help his feelings. It was kind of the Withers family to remember the educated Indian in his lonely solitude. Nophaie found cigarettes, matches, chocolate, raisins, a clasp knife, a little hand-axe, a large piece of tanned buckskin with needles and thread, and woollen socks and a flannel shirt. Withers had guessed his needs and had added luxuries.

Then with hasty fingers Nophaie opened the smallest packet that he somehow knew was from Marian. Inside the heavy paper was more paper, and inside that waterproof cloth, and inside this a silken scarf all neatly folded round a soft flat object. Nophaie unfolded the scarf to behold a large, clean, thick white envelope upon which had been written one word: Nophaie.

He put the letter aside, and opened the second packet, larger, flatter, more strongly wrapped, encased in pasteboard. He expected to find a photograph and was not disappointed. But before he opened the cover out dropped an envelope containing snap-shot pictures of Marian taken at Mesa with her own camera. The best picture was one of her riding the white mustang he had given her. They were all good, yet not one of them seemed like the image he had in memory. The desert was hard on Marian. But when Nophaie opened the large envelope he saw a beautiful likeness of the fair face he loved and remembered so well. This was a fine photograph, taken in Philadelphia, probably some time after he had left the East.

'Benow di cleash!' he murmured, and all the white flower-like fairness seemed to flash in a beautiful light from that pictured face. Gazing, he forgot everything for a while.

When he went back to his packages he found books, magazines, late newspapers, pads and pencils and envelopes, a small hunter's sewing kit, a box of medicines, bandages, candy, nuts and cakes, and last of all, a watch with radium numerals, and a buckskin fob decorated with Nopah buttons. She had not forgotten to include in all this loving munificence some token of the Indian. That thrilled him as nothing else had.

One by one he handled these gifts and pondered over the effect they had upon him. Beyond peradventure of doubt these established the connection between him and the world of white people. Eighteen years of his life, the forming and fixing period, had developed to such things as these, and not those of the red man. He might starve naked in a cave of the canyons, with nothing representative of the white race near him, but that could not change facts. He loved Marian Warner. Her gifts made him happy. The isolated solitudes of the desert were good for his soul and body, but they could never wholly satisfy.

CHAPTER 15

Nophaie carried Marian's letter to his favourite resting and dreaming place. Not on the heights did he care to read her message, but in the amber shadow of the Silent Walls.

'Dearest Nophaie:

'Greetings on your Christmas Day! I could not be happy without sending to you my greeting, and love, and my gifts. May these find you well. May they assure you at least of the constancy of Benow di cleash. I shall not be able even on Christmas Day to believe wholly in the spirit: "Peace on earth – good will to man". Not when the one I love, whom I know is worthy, lies hidden in the wilds, persecuted by men of my colour!

'If I could write you a whole volume I would never be able to crowd in all. My dismissal came quite some time after your visit. In fact, I ran the office until Blucher and Morgan came out of seclusion. Then I got the "steam-roller" all right and without my month's pay. I'm grateful for that, because it gives me an excuse to go back to the office, which I have done regularly since I came here to stay with the Paxtons. They are very kind to me, and allow me to pay my board. I help in the trading store sometimes and thus I keep up my study of the Indians. Here I get another angle on the reservation.

'As far as I am able to tell, nothing has yet leaked out in Mesa about that football match you had with Blucher and Morgan. The Indian police have returned from their search for you, I imagine. You will do well to lie low for awhile. There is a seething volcano under this particular part of the reservation. The Woltersons expect dismissal any day. All communication to Wolterson comes *through* the superintendent. Why, I could run this reservation better than it is run. The whole Indian Service, if judged by this arm of it, is merely a gigantic political machine. But that you know.

'I suspect that Blucher is greatly concerned about the possibility of the U.S. being drawn into war with Germany. There is indeed a grave possibility of that very thing. You will see the latest news in the papers I send. These came to-day with the mail-carrier from Flagerstown. Read them carefully. You may be a Nopah, but you are also an American. Blucher is all German. If war *is* declared the situation here on this reservation will be a terrible one. Think how to meet that, Nophaie.

'I have no plans. I am waiting. You may be sure I'll not leave the reservation. I might be taken off, but they'll have to carry me. This winter is no great problem. I need rest and I want to do some writing. Later, if nothing comes up here, I might go out to Kaidab. In the spring I hope to see you. I want you to know that I meant what I said in Blucher's office the day you confronted him and Morgan there. I would be happy to marry you and share what I have with you, and your life and work among your people. I have the means for a start. And we can work. I ask only that we spend some part of each year in California or the East. I have vanity enough not to let myself dry up in this desert air and blow away!

'Time and trouble change character, do they not? I am the stronger for what has come to me out here. The desert is terrible. It destroys and then builds. I never knew what light was – the wonderful sun – and wind and dust and heat – stars and night and silence – the great emptiness – until I came to the desert. Perhaps so with love!

'Somehow I will endure the long silence, for you must not risk writing me yet. I will dream of you – *see* you among the rocks. Always, as long as I live, rocks and walls of stone will have thrilling and sad significance for me.

'BENOW DI CLEASH.'

Benow di cleash loved him. She would marry him. She would share all she had as she would share his life. Live with him! Belong to him alone!

The fact was a staggering blow. Here under the accusing eyes of his silent walls he had feeling that no other place could inspire. Loneliness had augmented his hunger for a mate. Nature importuned him for her right. And suddenly Nophaie found himself stripped bare of all ideals, chivalries, duties, of the false sophistries of his education, of the useless fetters of his unbelief.

While he lay motionless on that mossy bank it seemed the elemental – the natural – the mindless automation of living flesh must win. There was nothing else in life. This staggering bundle of nerves, vessels, organs, blood, and bone that constituted his body had millions of cells, each one of which clamoured for its right to completion, expression, reproduction. Death to cell, organ, body, individual, but life to the species! This instinct that Nophaie strove to kill was the strangest of all forces in the universe.

One terrible moment Nophaie lay there under the walls that seemed to thunder the meaning of nature. Then he sprang up to force this living body of his, this vehicle he abhorred, this beating, burning frame of blood-veined muscle, into violent and sustained effort, into exhausting physical activity that must bring subjugation of the instincts which threatened his downfall. He must win now – in this hour – or lose for ever. If it was instinct that maddened him and instinct that he fought, it was also instinct that sent him out to move, to run, to climb.

He halted at his camp long enough to lay aside the precious letter from Benow di cleash. He did not want to soil that white paper with its beautiful and appalling words of love. All his life he must keep them. And he feared them now. Again the shuddering of his flesh, the burning of the marrow of his bones. Out he ran – straight for the notch of the canyon – with wild eyes on the white-towered wall of Nothsis Ahn. No Indian had ever surmounted that wall. But Nophaie would surmount it or perish in the attempt. To see afar over the desert, to pray and to absolve himself, the Indian had always climbed high.

Long after dark that night Nophaie dragged his bruised and weary body into camp, there to crawl into his bed and stretch his limbs, as if never to move them again. Sleep and rest, for days and nights, restored his strength, yet he knew that climb had been the supreme physical effort of his life. The strain of a hard football game had been as nothing. A hundred-mile run across the desert had been as nothing. Likewise Nophaie realised that he could never again climb the north wall of Nothsis Ahn. Powerful, fleet, sure, agile, enduring, keen-sighted, and Indian-sinewed as he was, these faculties did not alone account for that superhuman task. The very inspiration for the climb had receded somehow, dimmed and paled back into the secret and mystic springs of his nature. But as the days and nights multiplied in the shadow of the silent walls Nophaie learned that the noble proof of his love for Marian was not in surrender to it. He would not drag her down to his level. Utterly impossible for him was a life among white men. He had been wronged, robbed, deprived of his inheritance. He saw the incredible brutality and ruthlessness of white men towards his race. He saw that race vanishing. He was the Vanishing Indian. He had no God, no religion, no hope.

Days passed into weeks and weeks into months. Three times the Pahute came, and three times a white, thick letter stormed Nophaie's soul – yet left him stronger.

He measured the passing of winter by the roar of wind on the slope of Nothsis Ahn, by the circling back of the sun, by the earlier dawns, by the hot days and the peeping of frogs at nightfall. He lived that swiftly flying time in his simple camp tasks, in wandering and climbing as if the unattainable would one day be his, in dreaming of Marian and writing thoughts and experiences for her, in study of the nature of his stone-walled retreat.

124

The day came when a loud call awoke the drowsy echoes of the silent canyon. It startled Nophaie. That had not been the voice of an Indian. Had the long solitude worked upon his mind? Nophaie ran to the wide gateway between the red walls. He saw horses, mules with packs, an Indian – and then out from the shade of a cedar strode Withers, mopping his heated face.

'Howdy, Nophaie!' he said, with smile and earnest gaze. 'You look fine.'

Nophaie stirred to the warmth of the trader's close handclasp. He returned it and that was all his response. Utterance seemed difficult. Long had his voice been silent. Besides, Withers bore a look of intense strain. He was thinner, older. A suppressed passion seemed rampant in him.

'Come out of the sun,' asked Withers, turning. 'It's hot and I've ridden hard.'

Nophaie followed him to a seat on a flat rock in the shade. The moment seemed to hinge on strange events. The trader's presence might mean that which must add to Nophaie's burden.

'Throw saddles and packs right here,' said Withers to the Indian who had come with him. 'Nophaie, where is your horse?'

'Gone,' replied Nophaie. 'I have not seen him for a long time.'

'I figured on that and I fetched one for you.'

'Withers, why did you bring me a horse?' queried Nophaie, conscious of an inward tremor.

'Because I think you'll hit the trail back with me,' replied the trader significantly.

'Has anything happened to Marian?'

'Sure – a lot's happened. But she's O.K. – well and fine.'

'Withers, it's a long rough ride here. You've got a strong reason for coming yourself. Tell me.'

'*War!*' flashed Withers.

'Germany – and the United States?'

125

'Nophaie, you've said it!'

'Blucher – and the Indians?' Nophaie's voice was quick and ringing.

'I haven't a damned word to say about Blucher,' burst out Withers passionately. 'But I'll tell you a few facts outside the reservation. . . . Germany sunk the *Lusitania* with American men, women, and children aboard. . . . She has torpedoed American trading vessels – threatened and bullied President Wilson – insulted the American flag. . . . Then she sent submarines to our very shores. . . . The President and Congress have declared war!'

Nophaie recalled Marian's letters. Certain passages now seemed limned on his memory in letters of fire! – German militarism! Downfall of civilisation! Death of freedom! Slavery of Americans! – By every right and law and heritage he – Nophaie – was the first and best blood of America. The depths of his whole soul roused to strange fierce passions.

Withers held out a shaking hand.

'My son has gone,' he said, thickly. 'Already! . . . He did not wait for the draft.'

'Draft! What is that?'

'A new law. A war law. Every young man between twenty-one and thirty-one is called to army and navy – to fight for his country.'

'Will this draft affect the Indians?' queried Nophaie, sharply.

'No. They can't be drafted. But the government has appealed to all Indians to register. That means, as I understand it, an enrolling of the names and numbers of Indians – their horses and stock, so that the government can have this information for reference – for some use that is not clear to me. We're all drawn into the war – whites and Indians. But no Indian can be compelled to go to war.'

'Can they go if they want?'

'Yes. And the call is strong for Indians to enlist.'

'*I will go!*'

126

Withers forced that shaking hand down on Nophaie's shoulder, where it gripped hard. For an instant speech was beyond him. How strange the agitation of his rugged face! The unplumbed passions of the man had been upheaved.

'Nophaie, you don't have to enlist. You owe nothing to the people of the United States. They have wronged you.'

'I am an American,' replied Nophaie sonorously.

'I didn't come to ask you to go to war,' responded Withers, in earnest passion. 'But I came to tell you *this* . . . the Nopahs are being lied to. They do not understand the idea of registering. They are being made to believe it's a ruse, a trick to get their names, their thumb marks on paper. They are being deceived into believing this register is only another white man lie – and if they sign they can be drafted. . . . Nophaie, this tribe of yours numbers over twenty thousand. They must not be made to believe they can be unjustly driven to war. The truth must be told them. This false rumour of government treachery – this damned propaganda must not spread further.'

Nophaie understood why the trader's lips were sealed as to what he knew. Marian had prepared Nophaie for understanding of this fostering of hostility among the Indians.

'I will tell the Nopahs the truth,' he said. 'I will take Indians with me to war.'

CHAPTER 16

NOPHAIE bade a long farewell to his Canyon of Silent Walls. He and Withers made a record ride to the camp of the Pahutes, where they stayed overnight. Nophaie began his work there. None of the few Pahute men present, however, came within the prescribed limits of the war demands.

Another day brought Nophaie and the trader across the upland sage to the range of Etenia. The old Nopah had sons and relatives, and more horses and cattle than any other Indian in this quarter of the reservation. It was important that he be persuaded to accede to the act Withers had called registration.

Nophaie found himself received with a respect and deference. It augured well for the success of his new work among the Indians. Nophaie sought council with Etenia, which was granted; and the old Indian asked the honour of the trader's presence. Nophaie had gone over in mind an exhortation he believed to be honest, eloquent, and persuasive, and which he believed would appeal to the Indians. This he delivered to Etenia with all the force he could muster.

The old Nopah smoked in silence. He had been deeply impressed, and could not at once reply to such a strong discourse. At last he spoke.

'Nophaie sees with the mind of the white man – far and wide. He should sit in the councils of the Nopahs. Etenia believes and will register his name. He will sell cattle and horses to the government. He will say to his sons: "One of you shall go fight for America, for the white people, for the land where they keep us." Etenia will say his sons shall draw lots for him who is to go to war.'

That night Etenia had all his sons and relatives at his

hogan in honour of Nophaie and to hear him speak. He ordered a feast to which Withers was invited. They ate and made merry and sang. Then the old Nopah rose to address the assembly. He was solemn and austere, darkly impassive, chieftainly in his dignity.

'Sons – and sons of my people – Etenia has come to many years. He has worked hard and he is rich. He owes no white man so much as a silver button. He owes no Indian. . . . Etenia has not the wisdom of the gods. He cannot heal like the medicine men. Etenia's age makes him want to trust younger men. Therefore has he heeded Nophaie.

'Our white Father at Washington has declared war on a wicked people far across the broad water where the sun rises. These wicked people are warriors. They have long worked at the arts of war – they have long made guns and bullets and powder to prepare for war. . . . For three years now they have fought their neighbours – the white peoples who have sought to live in peace. And they are driving these good peoples out of their homes, killing men, women, and children. They will win the war unless our white Father at Washington sends many young warriors across the broad waters.

'Lies have been told us. Etenia's sons do not have to go to war. The white men who have spread such lies are snakes in the grass. Their forefathers belonged to that wicked people who practise war. They are not Americans. They are not friends of the Indian.

'Etenia's people are asked to register – to give their names to the government – and the number of their horses and cattle. Etenia believes Nophaie and the white trader. These men are not liars. Nophaie will ride over the ranges to carry truth to those who are being deceived. Etenia will register and he tells his sons and all Indians to follow in his footsteps. He will give one of his sons to go to war with Nophaie.'

Then Nophaie rose to make his address, deeply stirred by the words of Etenia. And with ringing voice he damned the evil force at work on the reservation, and brought home to the dark, still-faced Nopahs the truth of the real danger that menaced them. He did not appeal directly to the Indians to enlist. But he finished his speech with a trenchant statement of his own stand.

'Nophaie will go to war. Nophaie and all the Nopahs are the first of Americans. He will fight for them. And he will believe he is fighting no more for the white people than he is fighting for the Indian and his land.'

When lots were drawn among the sons of Etenia it turned out that the youngest, the favourite of the old Nopah, the joy of his declining years, must be the one to go with Nophaie.

'Etenia says it is well,' declared the father, with lofty pride.

At Kaidab there was a crowd of Indians, and an unrest and excitement totally new and strange to the trading post.

At the outset of his activities he encountered Shoie, the binder of evil spells on Indian women. Nophaie was about to pass him in contempt. But suddenly he halted. This Indian was young, strong, a keen scout, a wonderful breaker and tracker of horses. His mentality might be one to adopt itself readily to war. Nophaie meant to leave no stone unturned.

'Shoie, I am going to fight for the Americans,' he said, in the Nopah tongue. 'You are a warrior. Will you go with me?'

'Shoie will fight for Nophaie,' replied the Indian, with a gleam in his dark eyes.

For days Nophaie haunted the trading post and importuned the visiting Indians. His dogged efforts earned success, but nothing that satisfied him. Always he gained the attention and the respect now due him; only he encountered the wall of doubt that, once raised in an Indian's mind, was almost impossible to break down. One old Nopah said, 'All white men are liars!' Another Indian said, 'No white man can lie to me twice.'

The government idea of registration met with subtle and powerful check. Nophaie could not learn from any Indian just what was the content of the hostile propaganda. He guessed, however, that the idea of registering had been falsely represented to the Indians, and it was just such an idea that would stick in their minds.

Nophaie decided that it would be wise for him to ride out over the reservation and head off this German propaganda. He had intended that in any event, but now he saw he must make haste. Yet he was loath to abandon Kaidab with only seventeen Indian names promised for registration and but three for service. Withers' comment on this was significant.

'Nophaie, you've done well.'

At this juncture Nophaie received another letter from Marian, and it acted as a spur. Affairs were at white heat in Mesa – all relative to the war. Nophaie must do his utmost to counteract German influence among the Indians. Marian knew he would do his noblest and then go to France to fight for his country. She had spent some time at Flagerstown and was as well and strong as she had ever been. There now would surely be work for her on the reservation. The war had opened avenues for women. But whatever work fell to her lot, he was to understand that she would come to him, if he could not come to her, before he went to training camp. Somehow her words made Nophaie's heart swell with the thought of the part he could play for her in war.

Nophaie rode out into the desert on his mission, and few were the hogans he missed. It would be impossible for him to cover all of the reservation, and he did not have many weeks before he must report for service. But he rode fast, far, and late. Most of the Nopahs in that vicinity now had heard of his stand and were ready to listen to him. Every name added to his list strengthened his cause. Slowly the list grew and with it his influence.

One afternoon near sunset Nophaie reached a small trading post kept by a squaw-man. The last Indian Nophaie had inter-rogated had bidden him ride in haste to this post. Mustangs exceeding a score in number were standing haltered and loose before the squat red-stone house. But no Indians were in sight. Dismounting, Nophaie went to the door and looked in. He saw the backs and black-banded sombreros of a crowd of Indians all attentive to the presence of a white man sitting on the high counter. That white man was Jay Lord.

Nophaie stole in unobserved and kept behind the Indians.

'Indians, listen,' began Lord, in fluent Nopah. 'Blucher has sent me out all over the reservation to tell you not to register. Don't put your names or thumb marks on any paper. If you do your horses and cattle will be taken and you will *have* to go to war. There's no law to compel Indians to fight. You can't be forced to go. But if you sign papers – if you register – the government will have you bound. Then you've got to go. This register order is not what it seems. It's an old government trick to fool you. You've been fooled before. Listen to your real friends and don't register.'

When he concluded his harangue there followed an impressive silence. Then an old Nopah, lean and wrinkled and sombre, addressed the speaker.

'Let the white man tell why Blucher sends him. If the government lies to the Indians – to make warriors of them – then Blucher lies, too, for he is the government.'

'Blucher is a friend of the Nopahs,' replied Lord. 'He does not think the registration is honest. The government has made a law to *drive* young white men to war. It does not hesitate to *cheat* the Indians for the same reason.'

The ensuing silence of a moment seemed pregnant with the conviction of the Indians. Presently another of them moved forward. He leaped on the counter. He, too, was old, a scar-faced Indian, with fierce, dark mien. He shook a sinewy hand at the young men before him.

'Hagoie will kill any Nopah here who registers!' he thundered.

That appeared to end the speech-making, for all the Indians began to jabber excitedly. Nophaie took advantage of the moment to slip outdoors. Twilight had fallen. He walked to a corral near the house and sat down out of sight to wait for darkness and to think. He did not intend to let Lord get away from that post without being confronted. He had noticed that he was packing a gun. Therefore it would be policy to surprise him. Nophaie argued dispassionately that he had good cause to kill Lord aside from the possibility of self-defence.

In twos and threes the Indians came out of the trading post to mount their horses and ride away into the gloom of the desert. Soon Nophaie felt that he could venture close to the house. At an opportune moment he approached and leaned in the shadow of the stone wall. More Indians came out, until there appeared only a few left. Then, as Nophaie had hoped for, Jay Lord came out the door and strode towards his horse.

Nophaie glided after him. Then just as Lord reached for his bridle he must have heard something, for he stiffened. Nophaie pressed his gun against Lord's side and said low and sharp:

'Don't move your hands. If you do I'll kill you.'

'Nophay?' ejaculated Lord hoarsely.

'Yes – Nophaie.'

'Wal – what you want?'

'Lord, this talk of yours is *treason*,' went on Nophaie. 'Do you have to be told that by an *Indian*? . . . If I had time I could get Nopahs, and white men, too, who'd help me prove your guilt. But I want all my time left to undo your dirty work. I'm going to war – to fight for *your* country. . . . Now here, if you don't quit spreading these propaganda lies for Blucher I'll ride to Flagerstown and enlist. Then I'll come back on the reservation. I'll be an American soldier, outside the law. Blucher can't touch me or hold me. . . . And I'll kill you – Lord – I swear I will! . . . Do you believe me?'

'Wal, I reckon I do,' replied Lord gruffly. 'An' if you want to know, I'll give you a hunch I'm damn glad to be scared off this job.'

'Just the same – get on that horse and keep your back to me,' ordered Nophaie.

In another moment Lord, cursing under his breath, was in

the saddle. A hard, leathery thud and jangle attested to his use of spurs. The horse plunged away to be enveloped by the darkness.

To Nophaie's dismay he found that the farther he penetrated into this part of the reservation the colder were the Nopahs to his solicitations.

At length Nophaie headed his horse back towards the west and the country he knew best. One whole day he rode along the rim of a deep blue canyon, before he could cross. Many a day he went hungry, and slept where night overtook him.

At the Indian hogans east and south of Mesa Nophaie ran into conditions not heretofore experienced by him. As the taint of white civilisation began to be more pronounced here, so was the agitation incident to the war. Nophaie did not find the groups of excited Indians sympathetic to his cause. These Nopahs close to the borders of civilisation and the railroad were markedly different from the Nopahs far to the north. Rumours had been spread all over that section – enforcement of the draft, confiscation of stock and wool, seizing of all firearms. Blucher's minions had done their underhand job well. Nophaie saw more drunken Indians in little time than he had ever seen before in all his rides over the reservation. Many were selling wool to the traders, in a hurry to dispose of it. Prosperity was at its peak. But an ominous shadow lowered over the desert. The Indians seemed to feel it. Their work was neglected. Crowds of Indians rode into Flagerstown, to return with their minds chaotic. The fever of the whites communicated itself to the red men. The medicine men predicted dire troubles for the Nopahs.

Nophaie's passionate dream of leading thousands of Indians to war had to be dispelled. His tireless labours resulted in upward of two score of Nopahs signing their thumb marks to his paper. Word came to him from various sources that Indians were enlisting in the army, but he could not verify this until he got out of the desert. A terrible bitterness at the government

134

worked on him. In wartime what was the secret of holding a German spy to an important post, where he could undermine the faith of thousands of Indians who would have made great soldiers? Nophaie's heart burned with hatred for the German who had ruined the noblest opportunity that had ever confronted his people.

'I should have killed Blucher,' muttered Nophaie. 'No service I can render now will ever be one-thousandth as great as that would have been.'

Much as he yearned to see Marian, he was greatly relieved to learn from Paxton that she was in Flagerstown and would expect him there. She had left Nophaie a short note, telling him where to find her, and she entreated him not to tarry long at Mesa.

Nophaie had need of that entreaty. Never in his life before had he been the victim of the dark and terrible mood now fastened upon him. The wrath roused in him by the murder of Do etin and his ambushment by the Noki, and the tragedy of poor little Gekin Yashi, had not been the same as this, now so murky and hot in his soul. The idea of war had liberated something deep and latent in Nophaie.

Before sunset that day Nophaie was in Flagerstown and had dispatched a note to Marian. Before he started to meet her he had enlisted at the recruiting station and was a soldier of the United States army.

At the end of a street near the outskirts of town Nophaie found the number he was looking for. And as he mounted the porch of the little cottage Marian opened the door. Fair golden flash of face and hair! He did not see clearly, stumbling as he went in. Her voice sounded strange. Then they were alone in a little room with vague walls. Dread he had felt at prospect of this meeting, but he had not understood. He only wanted to spare her pain. This woman now, holding his hands, gazing with strained dark eyes of agony up at him, was remembered by her beloved fair face, but something in it was strange to him.

135

'Benow di cleash!' he said unsteadily.

'Nophaie – lover – my Indian! . . . You are going to war,' she whispered, and threw her arms round his neck.

Even as Nophaie bent to her white face and to her lips, he grasped at the meaning of her singular abandon. One word had been enough. War! And he pitied her, and loved her as never before, and understood her, and clasped her close, and kissed her until she sank against him, pale and spent. To him her kisses, with all their sweetness of fire, called to his own lips only an austerity of farewell. Long ago, in his Canyon of Silent Walls, he had fought his battle against love. Here he was as strong, tranquil, grave as she was weak and passionate.

'Nophaie – when do you – go away?' she whispered.

'To-night at ten.'

'Oh! – So soon? – But you go first to training camp?' she queried breathlessly.

'Yes.'

'You might not be sent abroad.'

'Benow di cleash, do not have false hopes. You *want* me to go to France. I'm fit now to fight. And it will not take long to make soldiers of my Nopahs.'

'That means the – the front line – the trenches – scout and sharpshooter duty – the most dangerous posts!' she cried, with a hand going to her mouth.

'Indians would not court the safe places, Benow di cleash. We are going – sixty-four Nopahs, most of whom I enlisted.'

Then he told her of his long rides and his importunities to beat Blucher's influence, and of his failure. She warmed to that, and in her anger at the treachery of the agent and her pride in Nophaie, she passed by the more poignant moment of this meeting.

'I knew he was pro-German,' she said, with flashing eyes. 'Yet, strange to say, he has strong friends here. Oh, this little town is out of its head. What must Philadelphia or New York be now?'

'If the Indians are excited, what must white men be?'

136

replied Nophaie. 'All this war feeling is bad, wild, terrible. But I have nothing to lose and everything to gain. I —'

'Nothing to – to – lose,' she cried, suddenly sobbing, and again her arms flashed round his neck.

'Nophaie, let me follow you to New York – to France.'

'Let you follow me! Why, Benow di cleash – I couldn't prevent you, but I implore against it.'

'I would never disobey you. Let me go. I can become a nurse – do Red Cross work – anything.'

'No. If you want to obey me – give me happiness – stay *here* and go on helping my people until I come back – or —'

'Don't say it,' she cried, and shut his lips with hers. 'I can't bear the thought. Not yet. Maybe some courage will come to me after you have gone. I love you, Nophaie. A million times more since I came out here to your country. The desert has changed me. Listen; after you leave I will go East for awhile. But I promise I will come back here and work – and wait.'

'All is well, Benow di cleash,' he said. 'I feel that I will come back. . . . Now let us go outside and walk. I cannot say good-bye to you inside a house.'

Gold and purple clouds attended the last steps of sunset – a magnificent panorama along the western slope of the mountain range. The warm summer air floated away, and the cool wind from the mountain took its place. The rosy afterglow of sunset faded into pale blue. A lonely star glimmered in the west. The great still pines grew black against the sky.

'Benow di cleash, when the Indian says at the end of his prayer, "All is well", he must mean just that. Your missionary never interprets any prayer as a submission to life, to nature. The white prayer is a fear of death – of what comes beyond. I have no fear of death, nor of what comes after – if anything *does* come. The only fear I have is for you – and such of my people as Gekin Yashi. So I bid you not be unhappy. If I live to come back to the reservation *then* you may have cause to be unhappy about me. For I know the war will bring misery and poverty and plague to my people. But be glad now that with all my misfortune I can rise above it and hate, and fight for you and your people. Love of you saved me from the dissolute life so strangely easy for the Indian among white people. It saved me to strive against my unbelief. And it has uplifted me to believe I may come somewhere near the noble Indian you have dreamed me.'

CHAPTER 17

AFTER Nophaie's departure Marian felt as if the end of all had come. She had not looked beyond this last meeting. And now with the poignant and stinging experiences in the past she seemed lost and broken-hearted. She fell into a terrible depression out of which she struggled with difficulty. The desert called her; the promise to Nophaie was a sacred obligation; but she could not at once return to her work among the Indians. She decided to go back East for awhile.

She did her bit in the way of buying and selling bonds, and in Y.M.C.A. and Red Cross work. But for her promise to Nophaie to go back to the reservation she would have gone, like so many young women, to extremes of war enthusiasm. The urge to go to France was something hard to resist.

Nophaie's letters were few and far between, and not what they had been out in the desert, but upon them Marian lived and sustained her hope. In September she went to the seashore to get away from the humidity and tainted air of the city, which, since her sojourn in the West, she could hardly endure. And she needed rest. She went to Cape May and haunted the places on the beach where she had been with Nophaie.

So time flew by, and autumn began to decline into winter. It took time for Marian to dispose of the little property she had, and following that came a letter from Nophaie telling her when he was to sail from New York to France. Marian went to New York in a vain hope of seeing him. But all she had of him was the sound of his voice over the telephone. For this she was unutterably grateful. The instant she had answered his 'hallo', he had called: 'Benow di cleash?' Then, shaking all over there in the little booth, she had listened to his brief words of love and farewell.

She was one of the throng of thousands of women on the Hoboken docks when the huge liner left her moorings. Thousands of faces of soldiers blurred in Marian's sight. Perhaps one of them was Nophaie. She waved to them and to him. She was only one of these thousands of women left behind to suffer and endure. This was harder for Marian than the farewell in Flagerstown.

Marian returned to Philadelphia with her spirit at lowest ebb and for once in her life fell prey to an apparently endless dejection. Besides, the cold, wet climate had a bad effect upon her after the dry, bracing desert. She suffered a spell of illness, and when she recovered from that she deemed it best to wait for spring before starting west.

In the spring Marian received a reply to a letter she had written Mrs. Wolterson:

'DEAR MARIAN,

'I am long indeed in replying to your most welcome and interesting letter. But you will forgive me, for my excuse is work, work, work. Imagine! out of six white people and thirty little Indian children *I* was the only one not down with influenza.

'We were transferred here, as you already know, and left Mesa without regret, except for our few true friends there. We are fortunate to be retained in the service at all. The wrong done my husband by Blucher and Morgan was not undone and never will be.

'Blucher, you will be glad to hear, had a sudden check to his open pro-Germanism. Something or somebody frightened him. My friends write me that his reaction to this fear, whatever it was, resulted in his applying himself to reservation work. But he will not last much longer as superintendent. He will get the "steam-roller".

'Here is a bit of news that comes closer to us. Gekin Yashi has again disappeared. Headquarters reported she had run

140

off. But my correspondent in Mesa does not believe it. No attempt was made to trace her. If she had run off she would have been tracked. Neither Rhur nor any of the policemen has left Mesa. I know what I think, and so does Robert.

'King Point is not at all like Mesa. I loved Mesa, despite what I suffered there. This place is high up on the desert, over seven thousand feet above sea-level. It is bleak, barren, bitter cold, and the winds are terrible. The snow last winter blew level with the sand. It did not fall! But there is beauty here. Great red bluffs, covered with cedars, and sand dunes for ever changing with the wind, and yellow mesas, and long white slopes of valley. But the solitude, the cold, and the mournful winds are dreadful. Influenza swooped down on us late in winter, a very fortunate circumstance. Had spring not come I believe the whole population of thirty-six would have been wiped out.

'I have no direct information regarding influenza ravages at other points on the reservation. But I understand it hit the Nopahs pretty hard. I never saw any disease like this. I dread the return of winter. Warm weather kills the germ or whatever spreads this sickness. If it should come early in winter I shudder to think what might happen out here on the reservation.

'You wrote in your letter of returning. We are glad to hear this news. Mrs. Withers wrote me that she had received a letter from Nophaie from France, and that he said he had seen you on the pier at Hoboken just before his ship sailed. But you did not see him! – How strangely things happen! . . . I have two brothers at the front in France. When I think of them I think of Nophaie.

'All good wishes to you, Marian, and let us hear from you.
'Sincerely,
'BEATRICE WOLTERSON.'

Marian went back to the Indian country prepared to work independently for the welfare of the Nopahs. At Flagerstown she rented a little cottage out near the pines, from which she could see the green slopes and grey peaks of the mountains. This time, with knowledge and means to set about her task, she provided a comfortable place to live in during absences from the desert.

Marian's first trip on the desert took her to King Point, where she spent a profitable day with the Woltersons. King Point was as cool and pleasant in summer as Flagerstown. Marian found instant antagonism in the head of the Indian school there, making any project of hers rather out of the question. Besides, there was no place to stay. The school was a small branch of the main system, and no Indians lived in the near vicinity. The missionary there had been stationed by Morgan. And his wife seemed to regard Marian with ill-disguised suspicion.

To Marian's regret, she found matters not happy for the Woltersons. Blucher's enmity had a long arm. Wolterson had encountered the same underhand tactics that had been operative at Mesa. Moreover, the altitude and the cold, and the poor quarters furnished by the government, had not improved his health. Marian advised him to leave the Indian service.

'Shore, I've got to,' he drawled, 'but I hate to quit just now. Looks like I'd be driven out.'

Before Marian left she received a suggestion from Wolterson that made her thoughtful. He told her about the little settlement of Nokis at Copenwashie, how they were growing poorer in water and land and had a hard winter ahead of them.

'Shore, they'll not be able to feed their stock,' said Wolterson.

'Why?' inquired Marian.

'Because they have less land than formerly and very little water. They can't raise enough alfalfa.'

'Why less land than formerly?'

'Friel and Morgan have got most of the Indians' land.'

'Oh, I remember. But *how* can they do that? It seems absolutely unbelievable to me.'

142

'Listen and I will tell you,' replied Wolterson. 'First Friel or Morgan selected the particular piece of ground he wanted. Then he got the superintendent to report to Washington that his land was not needed by the Indians. It was naturally the best piece of ground. The government granted the use of a little tract of land upon which a church might be built. Soon it was further reported that this was not sufficient for the missionary to raise garden and hay. Another tract was available and this was also turned over. After a time Friel applied for and received a patent to this land. Other patents are pending. With the land goes a supply of water for irrigating, and often in addition a good spring, and this much water is simply taken from the Indians. Water on the desert is limited. Last year was dry. This one may be drier. And there you are.'

'Well!' ejaculated Marian. 'So that is how these men acquire their lands!'

Marian had planned to go next to Kaidab, but influenced by the incentive of Wolterson's suggestion, and a dread of seeing just yet the beautiful sage uplands beloved by Nophaie, she decided first to look over the field at Copenwashie. The Paxtons at Mesa gave her a warm welcome, and between them, for the sake of a subterfuge that might be wise, they arranged a basket-and-blanket buying job for her.

Copenwashie lay down on the edge of the mesa two miles or more from the government post. At any time it was a barren, desolate outlook, and in summer under the leaden haze of heat it was surely mercilessly inhospitable to a white person.

The Nokis were agricultural in their pursuits, not nomads like the Nopahs. The two tribes had long been inimical to each other. One aged Noki woman, who was so old she did not know her age, had told Paxton she could remember when the Nopahs could ride down on the village and throw Nokis over the cliffs. Their houses were flat-roofed, built of stone and adobe, cool in summer and warm in winter, a very great improvement on the hogan of the wilder Nopah. In many cases rude corrals adjoined the houses. The several lanes of the village were, upon Marian's first visit, colourful and active with burros, dogs, chickens, cows, and Indian children. A keen tang of cedar smoke filled the air. It brought to Marian's mind the camp fire of the upland country. Thin curling columns of blue smoke rose from invisible holes or chimneys.

Marian went from door to door of these little low houses and asked for baskets. She saw stoves, beds, sewing-machines common to white households. The rooms she got a peep into were whitewashed and clean. The Nokis were short in stature, broad-faced, resembling a Japanese more than a Nopah, and the women all appeared to be heavy. They spoke a little English, but they were reserved and shy. Marian was hard to please in style of baskets, but she paid the price asked without haggling. Thus she carefully felt her way along the line of procedure she had adopted. When she left the village and ascended the slope to the level of Mesa she looked back.

Paxton had driven her down to Copenwashie, and said he did not consider it safe for her to walk. Opportunity to ride was infrequent, so Marian adjusted herself to a slow progress of passing the time and winning the confidence of the Nokis. But there were other demands upon her time – study, reading, writing letters, keeping in touch with all pertaining to the war. The heat of midday was, after all, not unendurable, and she got used to it, though she endeavoured to stay indoors during those hours. She hired the Indian mail-carrier, who remembered her, to carry her letters to Flagerstown and to do her errands. Three or four times a week she visited the Noki village. On each trip she bought baskets, and she always left candy and dolls and musical toys with the children. When a Noki woman asked her if she was a missionary Marian thought she had gained a point in her emphatic negative.

If happiness could have been hers it might have come to her here on the desert that had somehow changed her, and in the work she had chosen. But she could not be really happy.

144

Nophaie wrote but seldom. He was 'somewhere in France'. His letters were censored, and he wrote so little of himself. Marian lived in constant dread that she would never hear from him again – that he would be killed.

With the end of summer there seemed to be an end to the uneventful waiting monotony of her life.

Withers called for her one day and packed her off in his car to Kaidab. His wife was not very well and needed a change of climate, and wanted Marian to take a short trip with her to California. Marian gladly consented, and while preparations were under way for this journey she rode horseback, and climbed high on the black mesa to try to get a glimpse of Nophaie's country. All she could attain was sight of the red pinnacles of the monuments of the Valley of Gods. But she was grateful for that.

Withers found the time propitious for a short absence from Kaidab. His partner, Colman, said business would grow poorer instead of better. The decline of the Nopah's fortunes had begun. Price of wool had been steadily falling. There was no demand for baskets and blankets. The Indians had been prodigal of everything. There were no stores laid away. And they misunderstood the decline in price for their wool while the price of all the trader's wares soared higher.

'They're facing the hardest winter they ever had on this desert,' concluded Colman.

The last day of Marian's stay at Kaidab she prevailed upon Miss Withers to ride out and climb the highest point available. Withers sent one of his Indian riders with them. They had a long, hard, and glorious ride. From the brow of a great divide Marian saw the whole vast reach of the Valley of Gods – the red sentinels of the desert – lonely and grand against the haze of distance. She saw the dark, organ-shaped mesa under the shadow of which Nophaie had been born. Then far to the westward, up and up over the giant steps, she caught a glimpse of green-cedared and purple-saged uplands, and above them the huge dark dome of Nothsis Ahn.

This day had been full, poignant, resurging with the old flood of emotions. As Marian rode across the level stretch of grey desert before Kaidab the sunset was gilding the rims of the distant mesas. Rose and lilac hazed the breaks in the walls, and the waste of sand and grass waved away under a luminous golden light.

Withers was waiting at the gate for the riders. His face wore an excited, eager, and happy expression, such as Marian had never before seen there. What could have broken this intrepid Westerner's reserve? Marian experienced a sensation of weakness.

'Get down and come in,' he called. 'Come a-rustlin' now. I've got news from my boy.'

Marian tumbled off some way, and ran at the heels of Withers' daughter, who was crying: 'Oh! Dad's got a letter from Ted!'

So indeed it turned out to be. Mrs. Withers had been crying, but was now radiant. The trader fumbled over many sheets of paper, closely covered with writing.

'Sis, you can read all of this afterwards,' he was saying. 'Ted's all right. Fussin' because he won't see any real fight. He says what I told you all – the Huns are licked. WHOOPEE! . . . You know I wrote Ted months ago and asked him to find out about our Indians. I'd given up hoping. But he's found out a lot, and I'll read it. Marian, your Nophaie has got the D.S. medal! *What* do you know about that?'

Marian could not have spoken then to save her life. She seemed locked in sensation – mute in the sweetest, richest, fullest, most agonising moment of her life.

The trader fumbled over the sheets of paper. His fingers were not wholly steady.

'Here,' he began, 'this letter seems less cut up than any we've had. Ted writes: "I had some luck. Happened to run across a soldier – who'd been in the thick of the front-line battles with some of our Indians. What he had to say about

146

them was a-plenty. He knew Lo Blandy when he played college football. So it's a good guess Lo Blandy is our Nophaie. I got thick pronto with this soldier. His name is Munson. He hails from Vermont. He'd not only been in the front-line trenches with our Indians, but in the hospital with some of them. I've forgotten names and places, if he told me. This French lingo is sure hard for me. Munson said an officer told him there were thousands of American Indians in the service. That was news to me. It sure tickled me.

' "Well, there's more about Lo Blandy. Munson lay in the hospital with him, and found out he had been wounded four times, the last time seriously. But he seemed nearly well then. That was three weeks ago. Blandy – or Nophaie – was to be discharged and sent home as an invalid, incapacitated for further service. He had been in everything the war afforded except actual death. That seemed to miss him. Munson said Nophaie was indifferent to danger and pain. Shell-shock had affected him somewhat, and gassed lungs made him a probable consumptive. But to Munson he was certainly far from a physical wreck. I think Munson said Nophaie got into the great Chatoo-Therry (how'd you spell that?) mix-up, and that an officer gave him the D.S. right off his own breast. Sure some stunt for an officer, believe me!

' "Anyway, Nophaie, along with other Indians, must be on the way home by now. I'm sure glad. It simply was grand to hear what devils they were among the Germans. I can't remember ever caring a whoop about the Nopahs. But I've a hunch that a lot of Americans, including myself, haven't ever appreciated the red man.

' "My chance of plugging a Fritz has become slim indeed, and for that reason I'm sure homesick for you all, and the smell of cedar wood and sheep wool." '

CHAPTER 18

NEWS of the armistice did not reach Mesa until late in the afternoon of that memorable November day. It came from the lips of the mail-carrier. He was not credited. Paxton rushed to the telephone to call up Flagerstown, only to find the wire down. A crowd of Indians collected around the mail-carrier, and they all believed him. Only the whites were sceptical.

Marian went out through the store, down the stone steps, and into the crowd of Indians around the mail-carrier. Both Nokis and Nopahs formed that group. Excitement was rife. They jabbered in their low guttural speech. Marian smelled whisky. But resolutely forcing her way in, she got to the mail-carrier.

He was certainly in possession of his senses. Indeed, he was sombre, almost stern. If emotion held him it was deep set.

'What have you heard?' she asked in her own language.

'War over. Germans run – holler no more shoot – want make big council,' he replied.

'Who said so?'

'All come over wire. Heap talk over wire. . . . Men run round – get drunk – white squaws yell like hell. . . . All stop work – bells ring – big smoke pipe on lumber mill blow steam long time – no hear.'

And the Indian made significant motion to his ear, and then to his head, indication of his idea of a people with whirling brain.

Marian hurried back to the Paxtons.

'Friends, the Indian is telling the truth. There's a jubilee in Flagerstown. What else but peace could account for it?'

'Oh, it's too good to be true,' said Mrs. Paxton.

Just then Paxton's clerk came running in. He was pale, and appeared about to choke.

'Eckersall on the 'phone,' he blurted out. '*War over!* . . . Friel brought news – he and Leamon. They just got it from town. Everybody gone crazy.'

Eckersall was the government farmer down at Copenwashie and an old Westerner not given to hyperbole.

Paxton suddenly sat down as if glad for support. His wife hugged the little baby, and cried out, 'Thank God!'

December came, bleak and raw, but holding off on the inclement weather that made the desert an inhospitable place for white people. Influenza was reported by the authorities on widely separated parts of the desert. No effort was made to check the disease or to minister to any Indians except the school children. But it was not considered serious.

Marian awoke one day to a realisation that she had found favour with the Nokis. Long before she expected it she was welcome in the secluded homes of these strange desert people. After all, they were very human, very susceptible to kindness and goodness. They would accept charity and presents, but a material gift was no sure way to their hearts. Marian really did not discover this until after she had won them.

Then it became clear to her that she had been under as intelligent and careful a scrutiny as she had bent upon them. She was judged by what she said and did, and by developments that verified the appearance of her actions.

After Marian had acquainted herself with the actual condition of these Indians she set to work in her own way to help them. There were babies and old men going blind from trachoma; there were children with congenital hip-disease; there were always injured horsemen and sick housekeepers; last of all, the village was poor and growing poorer.

The war might be over, but its aftermath had just begun. There were signs that more than warranted the gloomy forebodings of Withers.

Marian never saw the government school doctor waste a ride down to Copenwashie. She brought a physician from Flagerstown. And his several visits, followed by her own ministrations, alleviated considerable distress. When the sceptical Nokis saw there was no aftermath from this, no obligation, nothing but the kindness of Benow di cleash, they subtly and almost imperceptibly changed. The old Nokis learned to relax their sombre faces in a slight smile; the children grew glad to see Marian, more for her presence than for gifts.

Naturally Marian's increasingly close relation to some of the Nokis resulted in their confidences. And by the middle of December most of the little tribe who owned horses and cattle, and especially all of the freighters, were hard pressed for feed for their stock. Marian lent money to some of the neediest. But the situation was not to be met by the little money she could spare. So she took up the matter with Eckersall.

'Reckon I seen it comin' all along,' was Eckersall's reply. 'The Nokis are in for a hell of a winter, if you'll excuse my talk, miss.'

'How much will it cost to buy hay for the winter?' asked Marian.

'Them freighters alone will eat up a thousand dollars before spring.'

'Oh, so much! I can't afford that.'

'Wal, sure you can't. An' what you are doin' more'n shows up this bunch.'

'Where can we get help?' went on Marian.

'Reckon I don't know. Have you any friends you could ask?'

'Hardly. I wonder if Withers could help us.'

'Withers! I should say not. Why, that trader is goin' broke on the Indians this winter. Mark my words. I met him at Red Sandy last week. An' I asked how about things out Kaidab way. He just threw up his hands.'

'Eckersall, who has all the alfalfa raised here this last summer?' queried Marian curiously.

150

'Friel has most of it.'

'Ah! And has Blucher any hay?'

'A-plenty. Some I raised an' the rest freighted from town.'

'Well, cannot the Indians get some of that hay?'

'Humph! They'll have to pay darned high for it. An' jest now is a bad time. Blucher is sore over the meat deal.'

'What is that?'

'Wal, miss, I'm only a government employee, an' I reckon I ought to keep my mouth shut. Sure I could trust you. But that's not the point. . . . I'll tell you what I'll do. I'll go to the agent an' make a strong talk for the Nokis.'

'Thank you, Eckersall. That's good of you. Maybe we can do something.'

But Marian's hopes were not high. And when from another source she learned the current talk about the meat deal she was even less sanguine. It appeared that as the winter advanced Blucher had solicited meat from the Nokis and Nopahs. But he would not pay over five dollars for a beef. As a result the Indians sold but little of their stock and the Indian school children had considerably less of a meat diet. Marian knew that the government advanced more money than offered by Blucher. But he refused to pay more than five dollars. It took no clever acumen to deduct why this was so and what he did with the difference.

Several days elapsed before Marian again saw Eckersall.

'Wal, me an' you are on the wrong side of the fence,' he complained ruefully, in reply to her eager query.

'How so?'

'We have a hankerin' for these poor devils of Indians. . . . Miss, I went to our German agent an' I made the speech of my life. I painted the woe of the Nokis an' the sufferin' of the horses as it was never done before. I told him that he made the Nokis freight supplies from town; that he didn't pay them enough; that these freighters had no other way to make a livin'. He said he hadn't any hay to spare at twenty dollars the

151

ton. Go to the missionary! . . . Wal, I went to Friel an' talked with him. An' he said *forty dollars* a ton! . . . The Nokis can't pay that. So I went back to Blucher an' railed at him again. He snapped at me: "If Friel wants forty dollars a ton for their hay, then the Indians will have to pay forty dollars!" '

The Nokis realised that their land was being gradually taken away from them, and this winter they had grown restive and morbid under the strain. In former years the Nokis had been allowed to raise alfalfa on a certain number of acres of the school farm, but this year that privilege had been taken from them. If the government was using all the hay raised and if the missionary demanded exorbitant prices for theirs, then all the Noki could do was to quit freighting supplies. For his horses had grown too weak to pull.

Winter came at last, biting, icy, and the desert became an open waste to dread. Day after day dark clouds rose, threatening storm.

Privation followed hard on the cold heels of winter, and many of the Noki families began to suffer. What with lack of food for man and beast the outlook was discouraging indeed. Marian bought stores of supplies from Paxton – who charged exactly what they had cost him – but these did not go far or long.

Then came the incident that heaped fuel on the fires of Noki resentment.

Friel had made a hurried trip to Flagerstown, where he learned that flour had gone up two dollars a hundredweight. It so happened that on his return trip he passed several Noki wagons going into Copenwashie to buy flour. Therefore, in possession of this information, he hurriedly drove to the trading posts at Copenwashie and Mesa, and bought all the flour the traders had, some two thousand pounds, at the old price.

Friel, before this incident, had won a universal dislike for himself. It then fell out that he was to go beyond the endurance of even these stoical Nokis.

He got permission from the agent to preach to the school children after they had assembled in the schoolroom each day. So he chose the first hour of the morning session and talked to the children about his interpretation of the Bible. The Nokis objected to Friel's taking the time from the school work to impose his doctrine upon them, and complained to the agent. Nothing was done. The Nokis grew more resentful. They roused dissension. Their activities caused reports to be made to the government, and an inspector was sent out. He ruled that the preaching during school hours be discontinued. But after he had gone Friel was seen to get audience with Morgan and Blucher, with the result that he kept up the preaching during the forbidden hour.

The Nokis held council over this turn of affairs and absolute usurpation of their rights. The chief himself came to Marian and asked her to read to him the ruling of the inspector. She did so, in Nopah and in English, both of which languages he understood.

'Benow di cleash, don't you think we ought to kill him?' asked the Noki.

Marian was shocked, and told him with all the force she could command that murder would only add to their troubles.

'Don't you think we ought to kill him?' the chief kept repeating to everything Marian said.

'No, no, you must not,' she protested. 'Try sending a delegation to face Friel. Show him the inspector's ruling and tell him you have had the white people read it.'

'Don't you think we ought to kill him?' was all the chief said.

But the next day, while Friel was preaching to the children, this delegation suggested by Marian assembled in front of the village.

It was a cold, lowering day, with wind sweeping down across the desert. The village had been swept clear of snow, except in the protected corners of stone walls. Marian had anticipated some untoward event, and she had borrowed a horse to ride down early. That trip had required something of fortitude. When she neared the village she saw Nokis riding in from the Red Sandy trail. And when she reached the dip of Mesa rim she had further cause for excitement.

The delegation contained all the male Nokis, and some of the other sex, with a plentiful addition of Nopahs. Marian's eyes gladdened at sight of the tall, graceful, picturesque Nopah riders, blanketed as they were. Manifestly there was something in the wind. The crowd was walking and riding towards the school. Marian followed. It was some distance, and all the way new riders fell in with the delegation. What surprised Marian and added to her excitement was the apparent fact that the Nopahs were going to take part in this protest. But to Marian it looked more ominous than a formal stating of objections. The Nokis meant to stop the preaching that they considered an imposition on the time and attention of the school children.

'Friel, come out!' shouted a clear voice in good English. It rang in Marian's ears. Unmistakably Indian, but was it Noki? Marian had to restrain a strange agitation. She convinced herself she was nervous and over-inclined to imaginings. But she felt that she could trust to her eyes, and she rode farther, to within one hundred feet of the school.

Friel did not appear promptly enough to please the Nokis. They began to shout. Someone pounded on the door. Then again the clear, high Indian voice pealed above the others, silencing them.

'Come out or we'll come in!'

The door opened and Friel appeared. His face was red. His figure, which resembled Morgan's, seemed instinct with intolerant authority. Yet in spite of this he was not at ease.

'What do you want?' he demanded.

'Get out. Quit preaching,' replied the leader, and from the crowd came shouts confirming his order.

'I won't!' yelled Friel furiously. 'Blucher gave me permission to preach. I'm going to do it.'

'Read the order from Washington.'

The man waved aside the paper flaunted in his face. It appeared to be in the hands of a short Noki, beside whom stood a tall Nopah. He wore a wide sombrero pulled down over his face. The crowd of Indians rode and pressed closer. A low hubbub of voices began to rise.

'Come. Go to Blucher. Let us hear what he says. Let us have understanding. You've got to stop preaching in school!'

'No!' exclaimed Friel hotly. 'I won't stop. And I won't go to Blucher.'

One of the mounted Nokis cast a lasso, the noose of which circled Friel's neck. The crowd shouted wildly.

'Haul him out!' yelled the leader.

Then the mounted Noki rode away from the school, drawing the lasso taut and dragging the missionary out through the crowd. His face was not now red. Both his hands clutched at the noose around his neck. Manifestly the intention had merely been to rope him and drag him into the presence of the agent. A wild young Noki, mounted on a spirited horse, pulled it up until its front hoofs pawed the air.

'*Hang him!*' this Indian yelled in Noki.

A roar broke from the crowd. In a twinkling the sombre spirit broke to let out the devil. The time was evil. Long had the war oppression and passion been dammed in the breasts of these Indians. Their wrongs burned for revenge. Some of their number were undoubtedly the worse for liquor. But one of this crowd recognised the peril to Friel and chose to divert it. He yelled piercingly and split the cordon of Indians closing round the missionary.

That piercing yell not only silenced the angry Nokis; it gave Marian the most startling shock of her life. She recognised that voice.

The tall Nopah reached Friel's side and his long arms grasped the taut lasso. With one powerful lunge he jerked

155

the Noki from his horse.

That tall form! That action! Marian thought she had lost her mind. Then the Nopah, in recovering from this exertion, rose to expose his face.

Nophaie! Marian screamed the name, but no sound left her lips. She reeled in her saddle. She clutched the pommel. A terrible uplift of her heart seemed to end in bursting gush of blood all over her.

One sweep of long arms sent the noose flying from Friel's neck. How ghastly and livid his face! He fell against the Indian, either in collapse or feigning faint.

The Indian braced Friel, shook him hard, hauled and pushed him through the crowd, and released him at the door of the school. Friel staggered in out of sight. When the Indian turned to face the crowd, tall, lithe, with singularly free stride, Marian assuredly recognised Nophaie. He began to push back members of that mob, once again pressing towards the schoolhouse. Other Indians, guided by his example, fell in line to avert further violence, and at length the whole mass, sullen and gesticulating, was forced back into the village.

It was afternoon and Marian waited in Paxton's sitting-room for Nophaie.

She had met Withers at the post. He had come to Mesa with Nophaie to take her back to Kaidab. They needed her there. Outside the dark day had grown colder and greyer. A snow-flurry whitened the ground. The wind mourned. Withers had said Nophaie looked well enough. No one could tell! He had reached the reservation from a point on the railroad east of Flagerstown. Two whole days! Forty-eight hours he had been on the desert without her knowledge! He had ridden down to the village to find her. God indeed had smiled on a missionary that day. A Nopah had saved his life.

Suddenly she heard a step. Soft, quick, padded sound of Indian moccasin! Her heart stopped beating. Nophaie entered. He was the Indian of her memories.

'Benow di cleash,' he said, in voice that was rich and happy.

She raised both arms and lips before strength left her. Then as he enveloped her she needed nothing but to feel. On woman's flash of sight – the keen, dark Indian face, thinner, finer, softening in its bronze – then she could see no more.

CHAPTER 19

A MODERATION of the severe January weather attended Marian's arrival at Kaidab.

Withers had said to her: 'We're a pretty discouraged outfit and we need a little of your sunshine. We all had the "flu" except Colman. Mrs. Withers isn't her old self yet. That's the worst of this queer sickness. It leaves half its victims with some infirmity. We're going to need you, and I reckon you'll be better off and shore happier at Kaidab. And if it's work you're looking for among these poor Indians – Ha! – I reckon you'll have enough. For this winter has started in a way to scare the daylights out of us.'

At first Marian did not see justification for the trader's grim statements. His wife was rather pale and weak, but she was getting well, and certainly was cheerful. The son was still in France, safe, now, at least, from the Germans. Colman had grown thin and somewhat sombre, yet appeared perfectly well. The Indian servants were identically the same as when Marian had last seen them. She felt that she must not, however, be over-sanguine as to the well-being of the Withers household. She sensed, rather than saw, an encroaching shadow.

Nophaie had no home now, except the open, and Withers forced him to accept room and board in his house. Marian was sure that one of the trader's needs of her was to help him keep Nophaie from going back to the hogans of his people, to do which in mid-winter would be fatal for him.

The afternoon of Marian's arrival at Kaidab was not without something of pleasure and happiness. The dark cloud hovered at the horizon of the mind. She herself brought cheer and gaiety, for she felt she certainly owed them that. Besides, the proximity of Nophaie made her more light-headed than she would have cared to confess.

Withers seemed to throw off cares of the present and forebodings of the future. He teased Marian and he kept coaxing Nophaie to tell something about the war. Marian added her entreaties to those of the trader. But Nophaie would not speak of himself. He told about the deaths of four of his Nopahs, all in action at the front, and each story had for Marian a singular tragic significance. Then he told about Shoie. American officers discovered late Shoie's remarkable gift for seeing or picking out weaknesses in the German front line, when they were driving. Nophaie said it was simply the Nopah's wonderful eyesight. At any rate Shoie was sent out on scout duty, by both day and night. He could hide himself on apparently level bare ground. He needed no more cover than a jackrabbit. He had the Indian's instinct for stealthiness.

From one of his scouting trips Shoie did not return. He was reported among the missing. But some time during the fourth night of his absence he crawled back to his own trenches. A sentry stumbled over him. Shoie could not talk, and appeared covered with blood, probably seriously wounded. Examination proved that he had been spiked to a wall through hands and feet, and his tongue had been cut out. As Shoie could not write his own language or understand much of the white man's, it was difficult to find out what had happened to him. Indians of his own kind at length pieced out the probable truth of his story. He had ventured too far and had been captured. The Germans had tried to force him to talk, or to make signs in regard to his regiment and trenches. They did not understand an Indian. Shoie made faces at them. They drove spikes through his hands and feet and left him to hang for a day. Then they tried again to make him tell what they wanted to know. Shoie stuck out his tongue at the intolerant Germans. They ordered his tongue cut out. And still they left him to hang. That night Shoie worked the spikes through his hands, then pulled out those that held his feet. And he crawled across

No Man's Land to his own trenches. He recovered from his injuries.

'Oh – monsters!' cried out Marian. 'Could they not have killed him?'

'Benow di cleash, the Huns were like Blucher,' replied Nophaie.

That was the only word he ever said against the Germans, the only time he ever spoke of them.

'And is Shoie here?' queried Marian eagerly.

'Wal, I reckon so,' replied Withers. 'He was in the store to-day, begging tobacco. Sure, it's a sight when he tries to talk. The Indians are more scared of him than ever. They think he has offended the evil spirits, who had his tongue cut out to punish him for casting spells. Something strange about what's happened to Shoie!'

'Withers, this will interest you particularly,' said Nophaie, 'as it deals directly with the Indian problem. . . . In New York I ran into one of my old college teachers. He remembered me well. Was not at all surprised to see me in Uncle Sam's uniform. And he was glad I had done something. He took me to dinner and we talked over my school days and football records. Asked me what I was going to do, and if I'd like a job. I told him I was going home to work with my people. That made him serious. He said: "The work needed among the American Indians now lies along the line of citizenship. This government reservation bureau is obsolete. The Indian myth is punctured. Whenever the Indians protest against attempts to civilise them it is owing to the influence of reservation officers and politicians who want to keep their easy pickings. These fakers encourage the belief that the Indian question is still serious, and that the government must still control them. Almost all the Indians have been born under bureau administration. They have been controlled by the political bureau. Most of them have learned to be dependent upon the government. They know nothing of white men's ways – which certainly is a black mark against the Indian Bureau.

' "The Indian in the war service brought to all intelligent and honest American thinkers something of vital significance. The Indians did not have to go to fight. They enlisted, perhaps ten thousand of them. Many were killed. They were in all branches of the service. I am absolutely certain that these Indian soldiers were not in sympathy with the bunko game of adopting American generals into the tribe. That was only some more of the politician's tricks to keep the reservations under government control and restrict the Indian to the desert.

' "And it is not only unjust to the Indian, but a detriment to the government and people. If never before the Indian has now earned a right to get out among white men if he wants to or to live free upon his unmolested land. If these Indian Bureau men were honest in their work to civilise Indians they would make them free and give them the rights of citizenship. Suppose the government restricted all the aliens and immigrants who settle in America. They would never become real Americans as most of them do.

' "The real good to the Indian has been subordinated to the main issue – and that is the salary of eight thousand government employees. It is a waste of money. Actually most of it is wasted!" '

'Nophaie, how would *you* decide the Indian problem?' asked Withers. 'I've been among Indians all my life. My wife knows Indians better than any other white person I've ever heard of. It's a problem with us. As old Etenia says, you've got a white mind and red blood. Tell us your angle.'

Nophaie leaned on the high mantel and poked his moccasined toe at a stick of wood fallen from the fire. He seemed tranquil and sad.

'I could solve the Indian problem. First I'd exclude missionaries like Morgan,' he replied, with a strange, dark bitterness. 'Then I'd give the Indian land and freedom. Let him work and live as he chose – send his children to school – move among white men and work with and for them. Let the Indians marry white women and Indian girls marry white

161

men. It would make for a more virile race. No people can overcome handicaps now imposed upon us. Not much can be done in the way of changing or improving the matured Indian. But he was good enough as he was. This Indian wants none of the white man's ways. He cares only for his desert and his people. He hates the idea of being dependent. Let him work or idle for himself. In time he would develop into a worker. The Indian children should be educated. Yes! But not taught to despise their parents and forgo their religion. Indian children would learn – even as I have learned. What ruined me was to make me an infidel. Let the Indian's religion alone. . . . The Indian is no different from a white man – except that he is closer to elemental life – to primitive instincts. Example of the white man's better ways would inevitably follow association. The Indian will absorb, if he is not cheated and driven. . . . I think the Golden Rule of the white men is their best religion. If they practised that the Indian problem would be easy.'

Late that night after the Withers family and others of their household had gone to bed, Marian sat awhile with Nophaie before the glowing embers in the fire-place.

This hour really was the happiest and most beautiful in its teaching of any she had ever spent with him. Much of his bitterness had vanished. If he had been great before he went to war, what was he now? Marian could only feel little, humble, adoring, before this strange composite of a man. For Marian he was now more of a lover than he had ever been. Marian trembled a little, fearful even in her hour of bliss. Why had he let down his Indian reserve? What did he know that she did not? If he had got rid of the scourge of his soul – his unbelief – he would have told her. But she would have divined that. Nophaie was at once closer to her than ever, yet farther away.

Bad news arrived next day, along with more raw, cloudy weather. Both white travellers and Nopah couriers reported increasing illness in the sections of desert they had traversed.

'It's come,' grated out Withers, sombre as an Indian.

The Indians were caught like rats in a trap. Their hogans were no places to fight influenza. Three months of growing poverty had suddenly culminated in a terrible situation. These Indians had saved no money. They had only horses, sheep, and corn. The price of wool fell to nothing. Withers managed to hold the best of the blanket weavers working at a loss to himself. He kept these families. And no Indian was turned away empty-handed from the store. Meat and corn were about all most of the Nopahs had to eat, and the time came when many of them did not have that. From a prosperous people they fell in six months to a starving people, at the mercy of a disease that seemed fatal to most. It killed them quickly. Those it did not kill it left blind or infirm or deaf.

In February hundreds died of the disease, within a radius of fifty miles of Kaidab. Whole families were taken. For many more days the sun did not shine, and the nights were black. The Indians thought the sun and moon had failed them. The medicine men prevailed upon them to believe that the only thing left to save them was the eating of horseflesh. Therefore they killed and ate great numbers of their best horses.

In the midst of this tragic time Withers received word that Gekin Yashi had fallen victim to the dread malady. A sick Indian rode in with the news, disclosing the whereabouts of the Little Beauty. She was married to Beeteia, a young Nopah chief who had been to France, but who had never given Withers a hint that might have cleared up the mystery of her disappearance.

'Just like a Nopah!' ejaculated the trader. 'Well, Gekin Yashi is down with "flu". It'll kill her – almost sure. Maybe we can get her out in time. Her husband's a fine Nopah. His hogan is somewhere up Nugi Canyon. I've sent Indians with horses to the mouth of the canyon. I'll take the car. Maybe I can drive up to the pass – maybe to the canyon. . . . Give me medicines and whisky.'

He had been talking to Colman and his wife. Marian sat beside the fire, startled and grieved into silence. Suddenly Nophaie entered, unfolding his blanket. His quirt hung on his wrist. Snowflakes gleamed on his sombrero.

'Ah! Here's Nophaie,' said Withers. 'I was hoping you'd get back. Have you heard about Gekin Yashi?'

'Yes. We must hurry. She is dying. And she has a baby.'

Marian leaped up, stung into action. 'Let me go with you?' she entreated.

Nophaie showed less willingness to take her than Withers. But Marian prevailed upon both of them, helped by Mrs. Withers.

The ride in the car, with a hot stone at her feet and heavy blankets round her and over her face, was not much for Marian to endure. But when she got into the saddle, headed towards the wind, it was a different matter.

The day was not far advanced, and the sky appeared divided into sections of lowering grey pall, broken purple clouds, and steely blue sky. The sun shone fitfully. At the outset the cold was not bitter, though the wind cut like a knife.

Neither sad errand nor inevitable discomfort could keep Marian from being responsible to other sensations. The mouth of Nugi Canyon yawned wide, a jagged, red-cliffed portal, specked with white snow-patches and black cedar trees. The bold faces of stone were glistening wet. A deep wash meandered out of the canyon. Cold and wintry as was the scene it held fascination for Marian; and though not in any degree so magnificent as Pahute Canyon it was impressive and beautiful. The towers stood up carved, cragged, creviced, yellow in the sun, red in the shade, white on the north summits.

Wide flats of greasewood sloped up gradually from the steep red-earth banks of the wash. A shallow muddy creek, lined with shelves of dust-coloured ice, wound between them. Riding across this creek, which had to be done several times, was an

164

ordeal for Marian. The ice shelves broke under the hoofs of the horses; and they had to trot through the water to keep from miring in quicksand. The steep trails up soft sandy banks further worried her. She had to grasp pommel and mane to hang on; and when she rode down, that was worse, because she slid far forward.

'Benow di cleash, do you see there is no feed for horses or sheep here?' asked Nophaie, turning once to wave his hand towards the flats. 'This used to be the most fertile of canyons. Two dry years! And do you see the empty hogans?'

Marian had not observed either of these features. But now the fact struck her forcibly. How bare the soil! Not a blade of bleached grass! Dead greasewood, grey as ashes, vied with the stunted cedars and a few scrubby oaks in relieving the barrenness of the canyon floor. Long slopes of yellow sand, spotted with horse tracks, ran up from the wash. Slopes of snow showed white in protected places on the north side.

Gradually the trail climbed, and gradually the canyon took on more of beauty and less of grandeur. The colours grew brighter. Patches of purple sage made wonderful contrast to the red cliffs. This softer aspect accentuated the loneliness and desolateness of the deserted hogans. How dark, haunting the eye-like doors, facing the east! No more did Indian rise to stand on his threshold, to see the sun break over the eastern ramparts! A melancholy stillness pervaded the atmosphere of this canyon. No sound, no living creature! Winter had locked the canyon in its grip, but there was more than winter to hold accountable for the solitude, the seeming death of life.

A grey moving cloud, low down, filling the canyon thickly as fog, came swooping down. It was a snow-squall. It obscured cliffs, side canyons, turrets, and towers, yet Marian could see its upper margin, a soft rolling grey mass, against the blue of sky.

When Withers rode up a bank, and into a clump of cedars to dismount before a hogan, Marian realised with a shock that she was at the end of the ride. She had forgotten its portent.

Nophaie slid off his horse, and dropping his blanket from his shoulders he bent his lofty form and entered the hogan. Withers ordered the two Indians he had brought with him to build a fire under the cedars.

'Get down and exercise a bit,' he said to Marian. 'They'll soon have a fire to warm you.'

'Won't – you let me see Gekin Yashi?' asked Marian, with hesitation.

'Yes – but wait,' he replied, and taking a saddlebag off his saddle he hurried into the hogan.

Marian had scarcely dismounted before the trader came out again, with a look on his face that made Marian's halting lips stiffen.

'Too late!' he ejaculated, a little huskily. 'Gekin Yashi died in the night. Beeteia's mother must have gone sometime yesterday. . . . And —'

'Someone said there was a – a baby,' faltered Marian, as the trader hesitated.

'Come here to the fire,' rejoined the practical Withers. 'You look blue. . . . Yes, there is a baby – and it's half white, as anyone could see. . . . It's about gone, too, breathing its last. I can't do anything but stay – and bury them.'

'Oh! Withers, let me go into the hogan?' asked Marian.

'What for? It's no sight for you – let alone the risk.'

'I'm not afraid of sight or risk. Please. I feel it's a duty. . . . I cared for Gekin Yashi.'

'Reckon that's one reason why I'd rather you remembered her as she used to be. . . . By God! every white man who has wronged an Indian girl should see Gekin Yashi now!'

'I will never forget the Little Beauty of the Nopahs,' murmured Marian sorrowfully.

'All right – you can go, but wait,' went on Withers. 'I want to tell you something. Beeteia was one of the best of the young Nopahs. He had loved Gekin Yashi since she was a kid. But she didn't care for him, and Do etin wouldn't make her marry him. She ran off from the school at Mesa – in her shame. For

Gekin Yashi was as good as she was pretty. But if she did run off it was made easy for her. Beeteia found her – his brother, who's with us, told me – and he took her home and married her. The half-white baby was welcome, too. Now he's in there holding on to the poor little dying beggar – as if it were his own.'

It took courage for Marian to walk up to that hogan and enter. The smouldering fire was almost out. She saw Nophaie sitting with bowed head beside a young Nopah – the counterpart of hundreds she had seen – who held a four-or five-months-old baby on his lap.

Even as Marian gazed an indefinable changing reached its culmination and set. She believed that had been the passing instant of life. Marian felt the drawing back of her instinctive self, repelled and chilled at heart.

Beyond these sitting Indians lay a blanketed form close to the hogan wall. It suggested the inanimate nature of stone. Snow had drifted in through the open framework of the hogan upon the folds of blanket. Behind Marian on the other side next the wall lay a slighter form, not wholly covered. Marian saw raven-black hair and shape of head she thought she recognised.

'Nophaie,' she whispered. 'This – this one must be Gekin Yashi.'

'Yes,' replied Nophaie, and rising he stripped back the blanket from the dead girl.

At once Marian recognised Gekin Yashi and yet did not know her. Could this be the face of a sixteen-year-old girl? Disease and death had distorted and blackened it, but this change was not alone what Marian imagined she saw. Gekin Yashi's songs and dreams and ideals had died before her flesh. She looked a matured, settled Indian wife. She had gone back to the Indian way of thought and feeling, sombre, mystic, without bitterness or hope, pagan or barbarian now, infinitely worse off for her contact with civilisation.

Marian fled out of the hogan, back to the fire under the

cedar. A horror possessed her – of she knew not what. Her own religion and faith rocked on its foundation. Plague and death were terrible, but not so terrible to contemplate as human nature, passion, hate, and life.

Her poignant reflections were interrupted by the voice of Withers inside the hogan.

'Nophaie, the baby is dead. Make Beeteia give it up. We've got to bury these Indians and beat it out of here pronto.'

Marian spread her cold and trembling hands to the fire. Somehow the trenchant words of the practical trader roused her out of the depths. Such men as Withers bore the greater burdens. He had kindness, sympathy, but he dealt with the cold hard facts. He was making himself a poor man for this Nopah tribe and working like a galley slave and risking his life. Through him Marian saw more of the truth. And it roused a revolt in her – against weakness and a too great leaning towards idealism and altruism – and for the moment against this stark and awful plague of influenza.

Nophaie might be taken. He would be if he kept riding the range day and night, exposing himself to both bitter weather and the disease. The fear struck at Marian's heart. It did not pass. It shook her and stormed her. If there were lioness instinct in her it raged then.

Withers strode out of the hogan, accompanied by the Indians.

'Get the tools,' he said, pointing to the pack he had brought.

Nophaie remained beside the hogan door where Beeteia leaned, a tragic and strangely striking figure. He seemed a groper in the dark. Trouble and grief burdened him, like weights. He did not seem to hear the earnest words of Nophaie or see the tall form before him. Marian sensed a terrible revolt in him.

Beyond the hogan, in a level patch of sage half circled by cedars, Withers set the two Indians to digging graves. Then the trader approached the hogan, and wielding an axe began to chop a hole through the earthen covering and interlaced poles beneath. Marian remembered that the dead bodies of Indians should not be taken out at the door. Manifestly, where it was possible, Withers did not spare himself in observing the customs of these people of the desert.

Beeteia turned away from Nophaie and went back to his dead. Marian called Nophaie to her, and she led him behind the clump of cedars, where the horses were nibbling at the sage. Nophaie's mind seemed clouded. She held his hand, endeavouring to quell her mounting excitement. The sun had come out momentarily, crowning the towers with gold. How deeply purple bloomed the sage!

'Benow di cleash, you should not have come,' said Nophaie regretfully.

'I'm glad. It has hurt me – done something more than that,' she replied. 'I was sick – sick deep in my soul. But I'm over it, I think . . . and now I want to talk.'

'Why – you're white – you're shaking!' he exclaimed.

'Is it any wonder? Nophaie, I love you – and I'm terror-stricken. . . . This awful plague!'

He did not reply, but his hands pressed hers closely and his eyes dilated. Marian had learned to sense in him the mystic, the Indian, when it stirred. She wrenched her hands free and then threw her arms around his neck. The action liberated and augmented the storm in her breast. What she had meant to express utterly, in her frenzy to save Nophaie and make him take her out of the desert, burst all bounds of woman's subtlety and deliberation. What she said or did in this mad moment of self-preservation she never realised. But she awakened to a terrifying consciousness that she had inflamed the savage in Nophaie.

He crushed her in his arms and bent to her face with eyes of black fire. He did not kiss her. That was not the Indian way. Tenderness, gentleness, love had no part in this response to her woman's allurement. His mastery was that of the primal man denied; his brutality went to the verge of serious injury to her. But for the glory of it – the sheer backward step to the

169

uttermost thrill of the senses – deep in the marrow of her bones – she would have screamed out in her pain. For he handled her, bent her, swung and lifted her, and flattened her body as might have a savage in sudden possession of a hitherto unconquerable and unattainable woman of the wilds.

Like a sack he threw her across her saddle, head and feet hanging. But Marian, once partially free of his iron arms, struggled and rose, and got into better position on her horse. She reeled against Nophaie. She could scarcely see. But she felt release from his grip. Something checked him, and his blurred face began to grow distinct – to come closer – until it pressed against her bosom.

'White woman – you'll make – an *Indian* of me,' he panted, in husky, spent passion.

It pierced Marian. What more strange, incomprehensible appeal could he have made? Yet how deep it struck! She – who had loved the nobility of him – to drag him from the heights! To use her physical charm, her power in supreme selfishness! It was damnable. It showed the inherent nature of the female. She abhorred it. Then came her struggle. Only the tragedy of this Indian man could ever have mastered the woman at that moment. Gekin Yashi, the poor demented Shoie, Beeteia and his unquenchable sense of loss, Do etin, and Maahasenie – these strange figures loomed beside Nophaie's. That was a terrible moment. She could work her will with Nophaie. Nature had made the man stronger, but the ultimate victory was woman's. But what of the soul? Could she deny it, crush it, repudiate it?

'Nophaie – forgive!' she whispered, encircling his head with her arms, and pressing it closer to her breast. 'I've been – beside myself. This plague – this death has made me a coward. And I tried to make you —'

'Benow di cleash, that'll be about all,' he said, raising his face, and he smiled through tears.

An hour later Withers' melancholy task had been completed. Beeteia refused to leave with the party. Marian's last sight of him was one she could never forget – the dark-faced Indian standing before the hogan he could never enter again, peering across the graves of his mother and wife, and the ill-gotten baby he had meant to father – across the grey sage flat to the blank walls of stone.

CHAPTER 20

THREE thousand Nopahs died of the plague, and from one end of the reservation to the other a stricken, bewildered, and crushed people bowed their heads. The exceedingly malignant form of the influenza and the superstitious convictions of the fatalistic Indians united to create a deadly medium. When spring came, with its warm sun, dissipating the strange wind of death, the Indians believed that the eating of horseflesh had saved them.

Slowly the clutch of fear loosed its possession of Marian's heart. Slowly the long spell of gloom yielded to a hope inspired by sunshine and a steady decline in the death-rate of Nopahs. Yet not wholly did her old spirit return. There was something ineradicable – vague, tenacious, inscrutable – something she felt every time Nophaie smiled at her.

They all worked to alleviate the sufferings of the Indians. If the trader had ever saved any money, he lost it all and more that winter. Marian's means had shrunken to almost nothing. Civilisation seemed far away, absorbed in its own problems. The affairs of the reservation moved on as always. And the little circle of white people at Kaidab lived true to something the Indians had inspired in them, forgotten by the outside world.

Nophaie had ridden to Oljato, and when he did not return the following day the nameless thing that was neither thought nor feeling laid its cold hand on Marian's soul.

She worked on Withers' accounts that day; she wrote long-neglected letters; she busied herself for an hour over a sadly depleted and worn wardrobe; she rode horseback, out to the rocky ridge above Kaidab, and strained her eyes on the

172

trail of Oljato.

But these energies did not allay her nervousness or quell the woman's sixth sense. She tried the trading post, which of late had been hard to bear. Hungry, gaunt Indians would come in and stand around, staring with great dark eyes until Withers or Colman gave them something to eat. It was a starved tribe now.

Outside it was growing cool. The sun had set, and there shone a ruddy effulgence over the tilted sections of wall in the west. Coyotes were wailing. Marian walked in the twilight. It seemed an immense and living thing, moving up out of the desert. An oppression weighed upon her. How dark and lonely the empty space out beyond! The stone-walled confines of the wasteland flung their menace at her thinking mind.

Withers appeared unusually quiet that night. His wife talked a little, in her low voice, grown like an Indian's. But the trader had not much to say. Marian sat beside the hearth, with eyes on the glowing white and gold embers. Suddenly she was startled out of her reveries.

'What was that?' she asked.

'Horse. Must be Nophaie,' replied the trader, as if relieved.

Marian sat still, listening. But she heard on a strange knocking at her heart. At length the door opened with a sweep. Nophaie! His eyes were those of an Indian, but his face seemed that of a white man. He staggered slightly as he closed the door behind him and leaned back against it. His whole body was in vibration, like that of an athlete about to leap. His piercing gaze left Marian's face to search the trader's.

'John – give me a room to die in!'

Withers gasped and sank back limp. His wife uttered a frightened and compassionate cry.

'*It's got me!*' whispered Nophaie.

Marian's terror voiced its divination of her nameless instinct.

'Oh, my God – Nophaie!' she screamed, and ran to him.

Nophaie reeled over her. Intense and terrible seemed the

173

strain of spirit over body. He clasped her shoulders – held her away from him.

'Benow di cleash, I should have been dead – hours ago. . . . But I had to see you. . . . I had to die as – a white man!'

Marian shuddered under the strange clasp of his hands. They burned through her blouse.

'White woman – saviour of Nophaie – go back to your people. . . . All – is – well!'

Then he collapsed against her and was caught by the trader. They half carried him to his room and laid him on the bed. Then began frantic ministrations in his behalf. The fire of his face, the marble pallor, the hurried pulse, the congested lungs, the labouring heart all proclaimed the dread plague.

Once in the dim lamplight, as Marian knelt beside the bed in agony, calling, 'Nophaie – Nophaie!' he opened his eyes – sombre, terrible, no longer piercing with his unquenchable spirit; and it seemed to her that a fleeting smile, the old beautiful light, veiled for an instant his tragic soul and blessed her.

Then it seemed to Marian that a foul black fiend began to thrust the life of Nophaie from her. It became a battle, all unconscious on the part of the victim. Poison fires sucked at his life's blood. This was not an illness – not a disease – but a wind of death that drove out the spirit and loosed devastating corruption upon the living flesh. Yet the vitality of the Indian held it at bay.

The trader entreated her to leave the bedside and at length dragged her back to the sitting-room. There Marian huddled down before the fire, racked with pangs. Oh! must this end in the futility of Nophaie's life and of her love? Mrs. Withers came and went, softly stepping, tender of hand, but she did not speak. The night wore on. Outside the wind rose, to mourn into the dead silence. The vines under the eaves rustled.

Sometime in the late hours Withers came to her and touched her gently.

'Marian,' he said huskily.

'Nophaie – he – is – gone?' whispered Marian, rising.

'No. Unconscious, but he's stronger – or I'm crazy. . . . I must tell you the strangest thing. Many of these Nopahs who died of this plague turned black. . . . Nophaie talked of turning *white*. He's out of his head. I was shocked. It's as strange as what he said, "John, give me a room to die in!" – Marian, it must mean he is true at the last – to the mind – the soul developed in him. Yet his life here was one endless struggle to be true to his birthright. But I don't believe Nophaie will die. He's past the crisis that kills so many. I never saw such strife of spirit against disease. It just can't kill him.'

Marian wrapped a blanket round her and went out into the night. The cold desert wind fanned her face and whipped her hair. Dawn was not far away. Her soul seemed flooded with infinite thankfulness. Perhaps the tremendous conflict in Nophaie was for more than life. Her belief in God told her so. She stood once more with Nophaie on the heights above the Marching Rocks! Had this dark proximity to death illumined his unbelief?

The desert was to be her home, in spirit and dream. Always it must be an irresistible influence for thought, for good, for the clarifying of life. She quivered with happiness to divine that always she was to see the upland sage of purple, the golden-crowned monuments asleep in the sunlight, the long green sweep and slope, the shadows of the silent walls – and somewhere against that background, the Indian Nophaie.

CHAPTER 21

NOPHAIE'S return to consciousness left him with fading memory of black hideous depths, where something inexplicable in him had overthrown demons.

He had expected that he would die, but now he knew he would live. Had he not welcomed death? A vast struggle had gone on within his physical being. Vaguely it seemed that he had been in terrible conflict with the devil over possession of his soul. Haunting, brooding thought of this strange thing occupied his waking hours and lingered in his dreams.

The satisfaction of the Witherses and the joy of Marian at his quick strides towards recovery gave Nophaie a melancholy happiness. They loved him. They did not recognise any barrier between him and Benow di cleash. Was there really a barrier? What was it? He spent hours trying to grasp the dim facts of former convictions, vows, duties. They eluded him. They grew dimmer. Something had happened to his soul or else the plague had left his mind impaired.

Nophaie was up and around on the fourth day after the crisis of his illness. He avoided contact with the Indians, and indeed with his white friends also as much as that was possible without being discourteous. And they in turn appeared to understand and help him. Yet always while he sat in the warm sun of the May mornings or walked under the greening cottonwoods Marian's eyes followed him. He felt them. And when he met her gaze at close hand there shone a beautiful glad light. It thrilled him, swelled his heart, yet he felt it to be a reckoning he must some time deal with.

In a few more days Nophaie's vigour had returned enough to warrant his leaving Kaidab. So, at an opportune moment, when he was alone with Withers and his wife and Marian, he spoke out about his plan.

'John, will you give me a pack of grain and a little grub?'

'What for?' queried the trader, in quick surprise.

'I want to ride off alone – into the sage – and the canyons,' replied Nophaie thoughtfully.

Marian left her seat beside the fire and came to him, quite pale, with wondering, darkening eyes.

'Nophaie, are you – strong enough?' she asked fearfully.

'It will cure or kill me,' he replied with a smile, and he took her hand.

'Reckon it's not a bad idea,' agreed Withers, more to his wife than to the others. She was silent, which in her meant acquiescence. Then he turned to Nophaie. 'You can have anything you want. When'll you go? To-morrow? I'll get your horse in or you can have one of mine.'

'Yes, I'll go at sunrise, before Benow di cleash is up,' returned Nophaie.

'You'll go off alone and stay alone?' queried the trader.

'Honest Injun,' replied Nophaie.

'Good. Reckon I don't mind telling you I'm worried a little,' went on Withers, running his hand through his tousled hair. 'Beeteia has begun to play hell with the Indians.'

'I knew that,' said Nophaie.

'Beeteia!' exclaimed Marian. 'Isn't that Gekin Yashi's husband? The young chief I saw up – there?'

'That's the Indian,' rejoined the trader.

'Beeteia has the best blood of the Nopahs,' interposed Mrs. Withers. 'He comes from the first clan. He's really a great chief.'

'Reckon that means more than I thought,' said her husband. 'He's inflaming the Indians against Morgan and Blucher. I hear he's – developed into a wonderful orator – anyway he has never got over Gekin Yashi's death. He is trying to get the Indians to rise against the whites. That's not new by any means here on the reservation. It probably will fizzle out, as

177

all the uprisings do. But it *might* not. I just don't like Beeteia's influence. Could he be stopped, Nophaie?'

'You would have to kill him,' replied Nophaie.

'Ahuh! – Well, all we can do is to hope nothing will come of it,' returned the trader, rising.

Mrs. Withers followed her husband out, leaving Nophaie alone with Marian. She still stood by his chair, looking down on him.

'Nophaie, where will you go?' she asked.

'I'll go to Naza.'

'So – far?' she ejaculated, with a little catch in her voice.

'It's not far for me.'

'But why Naza – if it's only loneliness – the sage and canyons you feel you need?' she went on earnestly.

Nophaie released her hand and put his arm round her waist. He felt a little shock go over her and then a long tremble. The sweetness and meaning of her presence had never been more potent. There seemed a difference in their relation – he could not tell what. That was another thing he must learn. He felt weaker, less able to hurt her.

'Benow di cleash, I'm not sure, but I believe I'm going to Naza because it's the greatest god of the Nopahs.'

'Oh – Nophaie!' she faltered. 'Are you still tortured? You told me how all the Nopah gods failed you. Even Nothsis Ahn was only a grey cold mountain, without voice or soul for you.'

'Yes, I remember, Marian,' returned Nophaie. 'But I don't seem to be tortured or driven, as I was when I climbed the north slope of Nothsis Ahn. It's something I can't explain. I don't even know that my desire to go is anything but physical. Yet I'm in strange mood. I want solitude. And somehow Naza calls. There's light – perhaps strength for me in those silent canyons.'

'Oh, if you could only find peace!' murmured Marian.

Nophaie left Kaidab before sunrise and rode out across the

desert in the grey melancholy dawn. The discordant bray of a burro was the only sound to break the silence.

From a rise of ground he turned in the saddle to look back at the trading post. A white object, fluttering from a dark window, caught his quick eye. Marian was waving good-bye to him. The act was something he might have expected. Reining in his horse on the height of ground, he watched for a long significant moment, while conflicting emotions burdened his heart. He would answer her surely. The little white hand-kerchief fluttered more vigorously. She saw that he was watching her. Then he answered with the slow sweeping gesture of an Indian who was going far across the ranges, to a place that beckoned him and from which he would soon return. He saw her face gleam from the window and he imagined the light upon it. Wheeling his horse, he rode down the other side of the ridge, out of sight of the post, and forced consciousness of Marian out of his mind.

He crossed the deep wash, and climbing out of it, and up the wind-scalloped and rain-carved rocky slope beyond he reached a point where he might have looked down upon Kaidab, but he faced ahead, eyes keen to catch the first sight of the great valley of monuments.

His destination for that day was the great pipe-organ mesa, now looming grandly ten miles farther on. It guarded the entrance to the sacred valley, where each separate monument was a god of the Nopahs. Fatigue and exhaustion wore upon Nophaie. But these were nothing. Only collapse or death itself could have halted him.

A soft grey twilight was creeping out from the red walls when Nophaie reached the spot where he had sat so many days as a boy, watching the sheep. It was a long ridge not far from the great butte. Grass and sage were thick there even as in his boyhood. The fragrance filled his nostrils, and memory, sad and sweet, flooded his mind. He found the flat red rock where he and his sister used to sit together. How long ago! She was dead. All his people were gone.

179

'The Indian in me speaks,' he soliloquised. 'It would have been better for me to have yielded to the plague. That hole in the wall was my home – this valley my playground. There are now no home, no kin, no play. The Indian's deeds are done. His glory and dream are gone. His sun has set. Those of him who survive the disease and drink and poverty forced upon him must inevitably be absorbed by the race that has destroyed him. Red blood into the white! It means the white race will gain and the Indian vanish. . . . Nophaie is not yet thirty, yet he feels old. He is ruined, he is lost. There is nothing left. He, too, should vanish. This spot should be his grave. Under the sage! . . . Death, sleep, rest, peace!'

But Nophaie's intelligence repudiated that Indian fatalism. It might be true to his instincts, but not to his mind. He was still young. The war had not destroyed him. The plague could not kill him. His body was tough as the desert cedar, his spirit as unquenchable as the light of the sun. Every day that he lived he could mitigate in some degree the misery of his race, if he chose. But his hatred – the hatred of Morgan and Blucher, of all the white men who had wronged the Indian – that was the cancer in his soul. Neither an instinctive Indian life, nor one governed by his white education, could be happy while that hate curdled his blood. Then flashed the uplifting thought that the love of Marian, given him with all the wondrous strength and generosity of a white woman's heart, should overcome his hate, compensate for all his sufferings, and raise him to a state far above revenge or bitterness. She had paid him for all personal wrongs done him by her people.

But here Nophaie felt the ignominy of his bitterness. His love for Benow di cleash, her love for him, did not seem to have power over that hate. Something more was needed. And suddenly he knew this was the meaning of his strange quest – of his pilgrimage to Naza.

In the rosy, silent dawn, with the sunrise at his back,

Nophaie rode into a dim and untrodden trail that climbed from the low country, up over the first red rampart, and on across a flat region of rocks and washes, up again and farther higher into the uplands of cedar, piñon, and sage. Behind him the great shafts and monuments rose out of the lowlands, continuing to a level where Nophaie rode in the same red stratum. Often he turned to gaze back, to see them dark and majestic against the white clouds.

He rode up a bare slope of rock, a gradual mile in ascent, wavy and hummocky with ridges and hills, canyons and holes, yet always bare yellow rock. Then he turned a great corner of wall and lost the backward view. To the fore was cedared flat, mile on mile, red-rocked and green-patched, stretching away to another wall. Nophaie rode at a trot now, and entered this flat belt, to come at length to a deep canyon. It yawned below him, half a mile in depth, with ragged slopes too precipitous for any but an Indian trail. Nophaie walked, leading the horse. The descent into the dry, hot canyon, under the ragged cliffs, and through the maze of great blocks of red rock, down into the region of coloured clay and dusty wash, was attended by a mounting joy. The old physical urge, the instinct of muscle achievement, the fighting of unknown forces by endurances, revived in Nophaie. Climbing the opposite side was travail. From the rim another flat stretched out endlessly towards the mountain wall, now vivid in colours of red, yellow, and violet.

Nophaie arrived at its base in the grey twilight, and made dry camp in a clump of cedars. He was getting away from the Indian reservation now. Little risk of meeting Indians from here on! Nophaie felt strange relief, that was almost shame. Was he running away from his race in more ways than one? Twenty-four hours and twice as many miles had removed him immeasurably from familiar scenes, from bound emotions. It began to be easier for him to hold long to the watching, listening, feeling, smelling perception that engendered happiness. If he could only abandon himself to that wholly! The

181

night was cold, the wind mourned in the cedars, the coyotes howled.

Next morning Nophaie climbed the bare-faced mountain wall that seemed insurmountable. It resembled a barrier of human passion. Spent, wet, and burning, he fell on the rim and panted. Ten days ago he had been abandoned by his tribe as a dead man! But his white friends had ministered unto him. His white sweetheart had prayed for his life. She had not confessed that; no one had told him, but he knew. He was alive. He was a man.

Nophaie laboured to his feet and mounted the horse. Something ineffably sweet and precious went fleeting over him. He could not grasp it.

Two days later Nophaie had crossed the uplands, travelled down under the north slope of the great mountain, down and down into the canyons.

It was summer down there. Hot, fragrant air moved in gentle winds. Green trees and grass and flowers and silver scale bordered the narrow red-walled lanes. Indian paint-brush added its vermilion and magenta to the colourful scene. Down and down Nophaie rode, under the gleaming walls, through sunlight and shade, along and across the murmuring rock-strewn brooks, beside banks of amber moss and white lilies, and through thickets of green oak and cottonwood, down at last into the well-remembered and beloved place where he had lived so long in loneliness and solitude – his Canyon of Silent Walls.

Nophaie rested there that night and the next day. In this deep canyon where water and grass were abundant Nophaie's horse profited by the stay. As for Nophaie, he strove valiantly to make the idle hours those of an Indian contented with natural things. Still he felt the swelling in him of a great wave of emotion. Something was about to burst within him, like the breaking of a dam. Yet he knew that with every moment he grew farther away from and above any passion similar to that of Beeteia's. A power of the working of which he was conscious, seemed to be gradually taking possession of his soul.

Starting on his pilgrimage again at sunset, Nophaie rode all night, down Naza Boco, the canyon in the far depths of which hid the great Nopah god.

That ride seemed a vigil. Daylight would have robbed it of some strange spiritual essence. The shadows under the mounting walls now showed black and again silver. The star-fired stream of blue sky above narrowed between the black rims, farther and higher as he rode down and down into the silent bowels of the rock-ribbed earth. Every hour augmented the sense of something grand, all sufficing, final, that awaited him at the end of his pilgrimage.

Dawn came with an almost imperceptible change from black to grey. Daylight followed slowly, reluctantly. It showed Nophaie the stupendously lofty walls of Naza Boco. Sunrise heralded its state by the red-gold crown on the rims. Gradually that gold crept down.

Nophaie rode round a rugged corner of wall to be halted by a shock.

Naza! The stone bridge – god of the Nopahs arched magnificently before him, gold against the deep-blue sky. He gazed spellbound for a long time, then rode on. At first it had seemed unreal. But grand as Naza towered there, it was only a red-stained, black-streaked, notched and cracked, seamed and scarred masterpiece of nature. Wind and rain, sand and water were the gods that had sculptured Naza. But for Nophaie the fact that his education enabled him to understand the working of these elements did not mitigate in his sight their infinite power.

He rode under the bridge, something that a Nopah had never done before him. The great walls did not crumble; the stream of blue sky did not darken; Nothsis Ahn, showing his black-and-white crown far above the notch of the canyon, did not thunder at Nophaie for what would have been a sacri-

183

lege for a Nopah. Nothing happened. The place was beautiful, lonely, silent, dry and fragrant, strangely grand.

Leisurely Nophaie unsaddled and unpacked in the shade of a cedar. Already the canyon was hot. The crystal amber water of the stream invited relief from thirst and heat.

Nophaie spent the long austere day watching the bridge from different angles, waiting for what was to happen to him.

Darkness fell. The low murmur of the stream seemed to emphasise the lonesomeness. At long intervals owls mourned their melancholy refrain. Naza stood up dark and triumphant, silhouetted against the sky, crowned with silver stars. Nophaie saw the Dipper turned upside down. By night the bridge gained something spectral and mysterious. Night augmented its grandeur.

Nophaie did not sleep. He never closed his eyes. Every moment hastened what he now divined to be an illumination of his mind.

Towards dawn a faint green light shone on the walls facing the south. The moon was rising. After a while the gleam grew stronger. Soon the shadow of the bridge curved on the opposite wall, and under the arch shone a dim moonlight, weird and beautiful.

After twenty-four hours of vigil under this shrine Nophaie prayed. With all the passion of his extremity he recalled the prayers of the Nophas, and spoke them aloud, standing erect, with face uplifted in the moonlight. His impulse had been mystic and uncontrollable. It came from the past, the dim memories of his childhood. It was the last dying flash of Indian mysticism and superstition. The honesty and yearning of it had no parallel in all the complex appeals of the past. But it left him cold. Despair chained his soul: then that strangely loosed its icy clutch. He was free. He realised it.

Naza! The Nopah god! Bridge of sandstone! It was there. How grand the walls it joined! Those walls had been cut by the flowing of water, by the blowing of wind. Thousands of millions of tons of sand had been eroded away – to leave Naza arched so magnificently there, as if imperishable. But it was not imperishable. It was doomed. It must fall or wear away. All that exceeding beauty of line and colour, that vastness of bulk, must in time pass away in tiny grains of sand, flowing down the murmuring stream.

Then to Nophaie came the secret of its great spell.

Not all beauty or grandeur or mystery or immensity! These were only a part of its enchantment. For Nophaie it spelled freedom. Its isolation and loneliness and solitude meant for him the uttermost peace. There dawned upon Nophaie the glory of nature. Just so long as he could stay there he would be free, all-satisfied. Even sorrow was sweet. Memory of his white sweetheart was exalting.

The world of man, race against race, the world of men and women, of strife and greed, of hate and lust, of injustice and sordidness, the materialism of the Great War and its horrible aftermath, the rush and fever and ferocity of the modern day with its jazz and licence and drink and blindness – with its paganism – these were not here in the grand shadow of Naza. No sharp wolfish faces of men limned against this silence! No beautiful painted faces of women! No picture of the Indian tribes, driven from the green pastures and running water of their forefathers, herded into the waste places of the earth! The white man had not yet made Naza an object of his destructiveness. Nothing of the diseased in mind and body, the distorted images of mankind, the incomprehensible stupidity, the stony indifference to nature and beauty and ideals and good – nothing of these here in this moon-blanched canyon.

As the sun cleared away the shadows of night, so the spell of Naza clarified Nophaie's mind of Indian superstition, of doubt and morbid fear. The tragic fate of the vanishing American, as he had nursed it to his sore heart, ceased to exist.

For Nophaie the still, sweet air of that canyon was charged. In this deserted, haunted hall of the earth, peace, faith, resurging life all came simply to him. The intimation of immortality – the imminence of God! That strife of soul, so long a struggle between the Indian superstitions of his youth and the white teachings forced upon him, ended for ever in his realisation of the Universal God of Indian and white man.

CHAPTER 22

At Kaidab trading post Marian watched the desert horizon with troubled eyes.

Nophaie had been absent for over two weeks. And developments of the last few days and nights had somewhat disrupted the even tenor of Withers' household. One night signal fires had suddenly blazed up on all the lofty points around Kaidab. Next day bands of Indians rode by, silent and grim, scarcely halting at the trading post. This latter fact was unprecedented. Even Mrs. Withers could not extract from any Indian what it was all about. But the trader said he did not need to be told.

'There'll be trouble at Mesa,' he said, with fire in his eye. 'Reckon I haven't seen the Indians like this since they killed my brother, years ago.'

In the afternoon he drove away in his car.

That night more fires burned. Marian went with Mrs. Withers and others of the post to see the wonderful spectacle of signal fires on Echo Peaks. To Marian it seemed that the heavens were aflame. She, like Mrs. Withers, was silent, not joining in the loud acclaim and awe of their companions. The trader's wife had lived her life among the Indians, and her face was an augury of calamity.

Next day many Nopahs trooped by the post. Then, with the advent of darkness, the magnificent panorama of fires was repeated. By midnight they burned out.

Marian lay sleepless in her dark little room. Some time late the hum of a motor-car thrilled her. Withers was returning, and the fact of his return seemed propitious. But the automobile hummed on by the post, at a high rate of speed. That dismayed Marian. It had never happened before. Kaidab was a stopping-place for every car, at any hour. Somehow this incident portended evil. Thereafter Marian slept fitfully and was harassed by fearful dreams.

Next morning she was on the verge of despair. Catastrophe had befallen Nophaie or he would have returned long ago. She connected his lengthy absence with this uprising of the Nopahs. Nevertheless, she scanned the desert horizon to the north, praying that she might see Nophaie ride into sight.

Her attention, however, was attracted to the other direction. The droning of another motor-car roused Marian to eagerness. She ran from the porch to the gate. Dust clouds were travelling swiftly along the road towards the post. Then they disappeared. Marian watched the point where the road turned over the ridge. Soon an open car shot into sight. She thought she recognised it. The driver appeared to neglect risk for the car or himself. Marian ran outside into the wide, open space before the trading post.

In a moment more she was confronted by a dust-begrimed Withers.

'Howdy, Marian!' he greeted her. 'Where's everybody? I shore drove some. But bad news travels fast on the desert, an' I wanted to beat it here.'

'Bad – news?' faltered Marian.

'Wal, I reckon,' he returned darkly. 'Come on in an' find my wife.'

'Nophaie! – Have you see *him*?' whispered Marian.

'See here, lass, you're white as a wheet. An' you're shakin' too. Wal, no wonder. But you've got to stand up under the worst. . . . They're bringin' Nophaie in Presbrey's car. He's alive – an' for all we could see he's unhurt. But he's in bad shape. Strange! Come, here's the wife. She looks scared, too.'

While Withers half led and half carried her into the living-room Marian fought desperately to ward off the sick, faint blackness that threatened to overcome her. Withers lowered her into a chair, and then stood erect to wipe his dusty face.

'Wal, wife, you're 'most as pale round the gills as Marian,' he began. Then, having cleaned his face, he heaved a great breath of relief and flopped into a chair. 'Listen. Beeteia's uprisin' flivvered worse than we'd have dared to hope for. Strange! Reckon it's the strangest thing in all my desert experience. . . . When I got to Mesa there was a mob, a thousand Nopahs and Nokis hanging around pow-wowin', waiting for Blucher an' Morgan. Luckily they'd gone away – to fire some poor devil off the reservation, I heard. The Indians thought they'd run away to Washington to get the soldiers. They cooled off. Then old Indians harangued them on the foolishness of this uprisin' business. Beeteia was hustled away to save him from arrest. So far so good!'

Withers paused to catch his breath, perhaps to choose words less calculated to startle the staring women.

'Last night we got word that Presbrey's post was to be burned,' went on the trader. 'I didn't believe it because Presbrey stands well with the Indians. But it worried me. So I left Mesa an' drove pronto for Presbrey's. Was shore relieved when I saw his tradin' post safe an sound. Presbrey met me, some excited for him. An' he told me Blucher, Morgan, an' Glendon had hid all night in his post an' had just left, takin' the old road over the ridge. Presbrey said a good many Indians had passed his post in three days. Yesterday they petered out, an' last night Blucher an' Morgan came.'

'I heard their car. I thought it was you returning,' spoke up Marian.

'Wal, while Presbrey an' me were talkin' three Nopahs rode up,' continued Withers. 'We figgered somethin' was wrong, an' finally got news that Shoie was at the mouth of the Nugi with a gang of Nopahs. They had been on their way to burn Presbrey's post an' were stopped by Nophaie. So, telling Presbrey to follow me, I hit only the high places. At the Nugi I found Shoie with some two hundred Indians. Nophaie was there, lying under a cedar beside my horse he'd evidently ridden to death. Shoie was with him. First off I thought Nophaie was dead. But he was alive, though exhausted almost to the last heart-beat. Shoie couldn't talk. The Indians were sullen. It took some time for me to piece together what this all meant. But I'm sure I got it figgered. Nophaie must have heard on the uplands that Shoie was bent on mischief. Wal, from the looks of my horse an' Nophaie I'd say there had been a wild ride. Anyway, Nophaie headed off Shoie, an' at least stopped the burnin' of Presbrey's post. Doesn't it have a strange look, when you think about Blucher an' Morgan bein' hid in that very tradin' post at that very hour? Shoie would have burned them alive. Nophaie is the only man who could have stopped Shoie.'

'Then – Nophaie saved their lives – Morgan – Blucher – Glendon?' burst out the trader's wife.

'Wal, I reckon,' replied Withers grimly. 'It's quite beyond me. . . . Presbrey came along soon an' we put Nophaie in his car, where there was more room. They'll be here presently.'

Mute and stifled, racked by a convulsion rising in her breast, Marian fled to her room and locked the door and pulled down the shades. She wanted it dark. She longed to hide herself from even her own sight.

Then in the gloom of the little adobe-walled room she succumbed to the fury of a woman once in her life reverting to primitive instincts. 'Oh, I could kill them – with my bare hands!' she panted. She had not known such black depths existed in her. She was worse than a mother bereft of her child. Her mood was to destroy. But for the collapse swiftly following, she might have done herself physical violence.

When her mind cleared she found herself lying on the bed, spent and dishevelled. Slowly she realised what havoc had been wrought in her by passion. She was amazed at this hitherto unknown self, but she made no apologies and suffered no regrets. In a revulsion of feeling that ensued she crept off the bed to her knees, and thanked God. For she divined that Nophaie's great deed had been dominated by the spirit of Christ. Nophaie had always been a man, and one prompted to swift, heroic, generous acts, but saving of the Mesa triumvirate from the vengeance of Gekin Yashi's race, from a horrible death by fire, could mean only that Nophaie's pilgrimage to Naza had saved his soul. She absolutely knew it.

A knock on the door interrupted her devotions

'Marian, come,' called Mrs. Withers. 'Nophaie is here.'

Leaping to her feet, Marian stood a moment, trembling and absorbed.

It took a few moments to smooth out hair and attire and erase somewhat the havoc of emotion from her face. Then she opened the door and stepped into the long hall. By the time she had traversed it and passed through the living-room to the door she was outwardly composed.

Through the green cottonwoods Marian espied a car in front of the gate, with an excited crowd around it. Mrs. Withers stood holding the gate open. Marian halted outside the door. She saw moccasined feet and long limbs encased in yellow corduroy slowly slipping down out of the car. Then she saw a silver-ornamented belt, and a garnet velveteen shirt. She recognised them. They were moving and her heart seemed to swell to bursting. Next Nophaie's dark face and bare black head emerged from the car. Withers and another man helped him out.

Marian's devouring gaze flew over him. His tall, lithe form, so instinct with grace and strength, seemed the same as always. Then she saw his face distinctly. There shone upon it a kind of dark radiance. He smiled at her. And suddenly all her icy terror and numb agony vanished. She ran to meet him to halt the little procession.

'Nophaie!' she said tremulously.

'All is well,' he replied.

Everything that was humanly possible was done for Nophaie. But it was manifest that he was dying and that the last flickering of his spirit had been held for this moment with the white girl.

She knelt beside him.

'Nophaie – your pilgrimage was not – in vain,' she asserted brokenly. 'You found —'

'Your God and my God – Benow di cleash,' he whispered,

191

a dark, mystic adoration in the gaze he fixed on her. 'Now all is well! . . . Now – all – is – well!'

Some hours later Marian stood in the doorway watching the Indians ride away into the sunset.

It was a magnificent, far-flung sunset, the whole west flaming with intense golden red that spread and paled far into the north.

Against this glorious background the Indians were riding away, in dense groups, in long straggling lines, in small parties, down to couples. It was an austere and sad pageant. The broken Indians and the weary mustangs passed slowly out upon the desert. Shoie, the tongueless, was the last to depart. It appeared that he turned with gleaming visage and gesture of denunciation. Far to the fore the dark forms, silhouetted against the pure gold of the horizon, began to vanish, as if indeed they had ridden into that beautiful, prophetic sky.

'It is – symbolic —' said Marian. 'They are vanishing – vanishing. Oh! Nopahs! . . . Only a question of swiftly flying time! My Nophaie – the warrior – gone before them! . . . It is well.'

At last only one Indian was left on the darkening horizon – the solitary Shoie – bent in his saddle, a melancholy figure, unreal and strange against that dying sunset – moving on, diminishing, fading, vanishing – vanishing.